CURSED DRAGON

DRAGON RISING SERIES, BOOK 4

TRUDI JAYE

WWW.TRUDIJAYEWRITES.COM

Cursed Dragon (Dragon Rising Series, book 4)

Published 20 February 2020 by Star Media Ltd

Copyright © 2020 by Star Media

Cover design: PCTC Design

 Created with Vellum

Hi, my name's Trudi Jaye and I've got a secret...

A secret society, that is.

Especially designed for people like you who love reading my books, the Trudi Jaye Secret Society is a place filled with magic and laughter, and most of all... free stories.

Everyone who joins the society, is given access to an ancient tome full of the stories, novellas, bonus epilogues, and deleted scenes from all the different Trudi Jaye series.

Called **The Shadow Archives,** you can access it by clicking the link below, and joining the secret society...

Join my secret society... if you dare!

www.trudijayewrites.com/shadow-archives

To Zoey. You are my everything.

1

Lifting my arm, I block the attack.

Magic shimmers around me.

Everything is bright and clear, a glorious high-definition array of sight and sound. The different greens of the trees are as clear as if I was standing right next to them, the insistent buzzing of the insects is an orchestra in my ears, the beaded sweat on Si's face like a multifaceted jewel.

But it doesn't matter, it's been too long. I haven't fought Si in months.

And I've forgotten how he likes to test my limits.

The first punch was just a decoy; he lands the real punch to my kidneys. I let out a painful breath and magic sizzles in my core. My senses sharpen, and I remember to focus on my opponent. Leaping out of the way of another strike, I raise my guard, and don't take my eyes off my mentor. We circle each other, both poised for attack.

He looks just the same. Tall, muscled, brown-skinned. Beautiful dark brown eyes that seem to see everything, even the stuff you don't want him noticing. His magic is like an aura around his body, shifting and swirling, intermingled with the glowing red grid of the spell web that covers him. He never ages, he's always calm, and he's always thinking a step ahead.

Jeff used to think five steps ahead, and that kept both of us on our toes.

We're in the middle of a forest. Tall trees loom all around the dirt training area, hiding us from the outside world. Birds sing from the branches, and I saw a doe wander to the edge of the clearing when we first arrived.

It should feel idyllic, but all it does is make me feel itchy. Nervous.

It's also the Chameleon stronghold. Si insisted we come here to train and to strategize. We're expecting my father to join us in another week or two, and then we'll be able to make plans for the future. I'm the spell web now. Apparently that means I need to be prepared.

The fiery magic from the spell web, now coiled inside me, is ready to strike out, to end this fight here and now. And I totally could. Instead, I hold it in place, unwilling to use it just to win a training fight. I'm conscious that every time I use the spell web, I'm stealing magic from another super somewhere. I refuse to let that happen just to win against Si.

The sun beats down on us from high in the sky, and I wonder if there's a way to tell where we are based on its position. We've been living here for a week, and I still have no idea of the location. They made us wear face masks when they picked us up. We drove for at least an hour, blindfolded and full of curiosity.

Just at that moment—almost like he could see I wasn't paying full attention—Si lunges forward, striking in a quick three-punch move. I manage to block the first two, then catch the third on my side. I grunt in response, and the spell web shimmers around me.

Si insisted that both Seth and I train with him, and he's not going easy on me just because I've got the spell web inside me.

In fact the opposite.

I think he's trying to train me to expect anything, to defend the spell web with everything I have.

And I mean *everything*.

He lunges at me, fakes to the right and then goes left. I'm ready for him this time, and his strike goes wide. I'm using my natural dragon strength and speed against him now.

But he just gets a glint in his eyes and amps up his fighting. He starts moving faster, his limbs blurred. I should have known he was holding back on me all these years. He lands another strike to my ribs, and I'm knocked backward onto my butt. A mist swirls around me, my magic gathering, wanting desperately to strike back at him. But I control it. I pull myself back to my feet, shake it out, and keep bouncing on my toes, looking for my opportunity.

"Hey, you two! Water break." Seth's voice is a welcome relief. But I don't take my eyes off Si until he drops his guard and bows to me.

I return the bow, still watching him warily. I don't quite trust him not to come at me and tell me that my enemies don't take drink breaks.

But he walks over to Seth and takes the glass from him, not saying a word.

I follow him and gratefully take the second glass, taking a big gulp of the cool liquid. Sweat is pouring off me, and my fighting *gi* is soaked. "Thanks, Seth. That's so good."

"I take it that our holiday is over?" asks Seth, his eyebrows raised. "It must be my turn to take a beating." His hair, which used to be regulation short, now hangs down over his cheeks, and his eye patch covers part of the long scar running down the side of his face.

He looks a little like a pirate. I love it.

"Mei needs to build up her stamina. And work on her thinking," says Si.

"Hey, I have plenty of stamina," I say, scowling over at him.

"Then how come I managed to land a punch? You would never have allowed that in the old days."

"The old days being a few months ago?"

"Yes. Before you had your dragon abilities to lean on. You can't rely on being the biggest predator in the room. Look what happened to the dragons of old. They were taken out by a coalition of far weaker supers."

"Is this like the gun argument?"

"This is precisely like the gun argument."

I turn to Seth. "Watch out, he's going to be twice as hard on you, just because you're a phoenix now."

Seth grins slyly at Si. "He's never fought me before. He doesn't know my old abilities."

"That's where you're wrong," says Si smoothly. "Before I agreed to let you come and guard Mei, Jeff and I viewed your fighting videos from the training facility. I know exactly what you're capable of."

Seth groans. "Seriously?"

"Yes. You were weak in some areas, but we saw potential that I could work with."

I smirk at Seth. "You had potential."

He mock-growls at me, before breaking out into a grin. "Better than no potential, I suppose."

Si claps his hands together. "Okay, no more break time. Mei, stay here and give Seth pointers. Seth, into the ring." Si is all business, his movements effortlessly athletic as he strides into the dirt training area.

The two fighters—one young, one ageless—circle each other. Si is strong and fluid, the far more experienced fighter. But Seth's phoenix side glows through, even when he's in his human form. His spell web is stronger these days too, glowing red like a warning to other supers of his powers. Added to that, he has a raw determination and a fierce concentration that might just save him.

Or at least mean he doesn't fall flat on his face in the first five seconds.

Si hits out first, faking one way and then punching Seth in the stomach. Seth grunts, but says nothing. Seth's guard is up, his form is good.

He's fast, strong, and experienced. For a SIG agent.

But he's never fought someone like Si. The Chameleon whips around the ring, punching and kicking until Seth is sweating and red-faced. His eye has turned to fire, the phoenix rising inside him as he takes more and more of a beating.

The spell web surges inside me in response, sending tingles across my skin. I shiver even as I hold the magic in check. There's nothing I can do for Seth right now.

He has to learn to fight Si all on his own.

2

S eth surges forward, punching and then kicking at Si. Both attempts go wide, and Seth stumbles past his opponent, his breath heaving.

He's leaning over, struggling for breath when Si slams his arm down across Seth's back, making the younger man grunt in pain.

Si slams a front kick into Seth's butt, and Seth is launched toward the ground, only just getting his hands up in time to save himself from slamming his face into the dirt. He stays down a moment too long. Si goes over to him and holds out one arm.

I wince. This is an old trick of Si's.

Seth holds out one weary arm and grasps Si's proffered hand. As soon as they've clasped hands tightly, Si pulls an unsuspecting Seth to his feet, then slams his other fist into Seth's kidneys. Then he raises his knee and, in one quick move, slams it into Seth's groin.

Seth howls in pain and bends over, holding himself. His face and neck have gone a reddish purple.

"Never trust your opponent," says Si. "Even when it

seems like they're helping you. Your enemies will never help you."

Seth looks up at Si, and the flames in his one visible eye have taken over. Anger radiates from every pore, and flames are developing over his skin. His phoenix magic is spilling out into the ring. Seth snarls.

Si narrows his eyes, and his body is immediately covered in the thick scales that protect him from dragon fire—and presumably phoenix fire. It's a trick that only the most powerful and experienced Chameleon shifters can manage —staying human and using only one part of their Chameleon self as protection.

"Don't get angry in a fight. It's the fastest way to lose," says Si, never taking his eyes from Seth.

Seth pulls himself to standing. The flames over his body are burning brighter now. My dragon magic quivers in response. I can't help it. As much as I know that it's better to be cool and calm in a fight, there's something in me that really appreciates Seth when he's like this.

He's magnificent when he's angry.

Seth takes a step closer to Si, and suddenly his wings appear behind him, made of nothing more than fire and air. He's close to turning, and he's angry as hell.

"Turning isn't the way to win this fight," says Si. "Just like Mei, you can't rely on your magic. You need to use your head. To think your way through a fight. It's the only way to win."

Seth narrows his eye and seems to consider it for a moment. His wings disappear, and he loosens his stance. Si launches himself forward, slamming his hand at Seth's face. Seth moves out of the way—just—and takes the brunt of the force on his arm. He turns quickly and tries to get a hit onto Si's side, missing by a mile.

The older Chameleon is still the better fighter. Si moves impossibly fast, his feet blurred, and suddenly Seth is face-down on the ground, his back crunched down under Si's knee, one arm bent painfully back and in the air.

I can feel Seth's rage from where I'm sitting cross-legged at the edge of the dirt. The spell web is swirling agitatedly around me, like it wants to get out. My dragon magic is humming in satisfaction, somehow enjoying the spectacle. I'm not sure if it's the violence, or simply how close Seth is to changing that pleases that part of me so much.

Seth growls, and his phoenix wings appear again. They burn right through Si, who snarls and steps back, flicking his hands as if trying to stave off a burn. Seth surges up, and this time he's so close to changing, his entire body is covered in flames; his wings are behind him, and his good eye is full of fire mixed with the sharp tawny shade of his other self.

With a shake of his head, and a radiant flash of sparks that hit the dirt and spring away, Seth turns.

His phoenix form emerges out of his human self with a fluidity and grace that takes my breath away. Magic dances inside me in response to his awesome display. The air becomes burning hot, and sparks fill the space between Seth and Si.

The Chameleon takes a step backward, holding up his hands in surrender. "That's enough, Seth. We're done here today. You need to learn control, or you'll never win."

Seth screeches, and I hear the thought as clearly as if he spoke it: *Am I not winning this fight right now?*

"You might win a fight, maybe even a battle, but you will never win the war." Si just holds his stance, and watches Seth, too experienced to turn his back on the younger man.

Seth screeches again and takes a mighty step forward, until he's right up in Si's face. His wings are swept wide, and one of his enormous talons is raised as if to attack Si. Suddenly, I'm not sure how in control of himself Seth is. His expression seems wild, untamable, and fear surges to the surface. Would he hurt Si?

Standing, I race over. "Seth. Look at me. Stand down. It's over. Your fight is over." My spell web magic swirls around us, and I finally let it free, trying to dampen down Seth's rage to manageable levels. Seth's head turns to me, his tawny eye at first battling with the magic from the spell web. He moves, and for a moment, it seems like he might attack me instead. Instead he looms over my human form, fiery and fierce, willing me to back off and let him finish what he started.

Except I can't.

I have to help him control himself. I curl my hands into tight fists, plant my feet into the ground, and glare up at him. "The fight is over," I repeat to him. Our magic goes head to head, dust swirling around us as Seth's phoenix self rages at me.

Suddenly, a sharp pain, like a thousand giant needles, stabs its way down through my body, from head to foot. My whole body goes taut with the unexpected agony of it. The pain is everywhere inside me, sharp and stinging. I stare at Seth, shocked that he's attacking me like this.

But it's different to his burning magic. The pain isn't from the heat of his phoenix soul. It's agonizing—tiny pinpricks of pain covering my entire body, like fire ants who're each attacking individually. And they've brought some glass shards to scrape around over me. And maybe there's a bear or two sharpening their claws down my body.

This is something or someone I don't recognize attacking me from the inside out.

Bright light burns my eyes, and all the noise in the area

has been turned up, making my ear drums burst with pain. I can't hold in my scream. My legs turn to Jell-O under me, and I collapse.

Si reaches me before I hit the ground. Moments later, Seth kneels on my other side, his now-human face creased with worry.

"What's happening? What's wrong, Mei?" Seth looks around us, as if he's searching for a sniper. It's probably what it looked like.

"Attacking... me," I manage. The pain is still rampaging through my body. I'm gasping in breaths like I'm out of air. I can't smell anything strange or see anyone around us who might be attacking me. "Someone's... using... magic against... me," I gasp out.

3

I can't think, see, or understand.

Pain is all I know. I close my eyes, and I'm surrounded by a darkness so deep it's never-ending. It seems to stretch in front of me, around me, in every direction, with no end.

I scream again.

I can't help myself. I've never felt anything like this, not even when I transformed into a dragon for the first time. I'm being attacked, and I can't defend myself.

I don't even know who's attacking me. Or from where.

I have no enemy to fight, no way to end this.

The pain is too intense, too much to handle. Without thinking, I try to pull on the power of the spell web. I need its protection. I don't know the full repercussions of using it, and right now I don't care. But even the spell web is locked down. The swirling magic that was there only a second ago is gone. I can't access its power. Fear worms its way through my body. If I can't use my magic against this enemy, how will I defeat it?

And then, as suddenly as it started, the pain ends.

I take a gasping breath, not quite ready to believe the attack is over. Holding myself tense for it to all start again.

Another breath.

I'm still okay. I open my eyes. Both men are kneeling next to me, their expressions anxious.

Seth reaches out and touches my cheek with gentle fingers. I lean into his hand, gathering strength from his fiery phoenix warmth.

"You okay?" he asks softly.

I manage a nod. "It's gone."

"What was it? Where did it come from?" Seth's voice is raw.

"I don't know. I was fine... and then I wasn't."

Si shakes his head. "This is why we must prepare you. There are many who wish to harm you. Many who still want the spell web gone."

"I couldn't fight it," I whisper. My body feels limp, and fear gnaws at my insides.

"Next time, you will be more prepared."

Next time? I don't want to ever experience that pain again. I shake my head, as if I can ward it away just like that.

"We must prepare as if it will happen again," says Si, his voice a warning.

I glare up at him. "But what kind of attack was it? What kind of supernatural could do that to me?" My first thought is Vincent... but he's dead. Carrick and Elena are in charge of the Earthbound compound and the old Earthbound records now.

"I can show you some old Chameleon tricks to create a fortress in your mind," says Si. "To protect against attacks inside your head."

"I don't think I can control it," I say, and my voice

wobbles. My dragon self wants to growl and rage, but right now, my human side is in control.

"You can, and you will. This is about more than just you now, Mei. This is everyone." Si's expression is stern, his dark eyes flashing at me. This is more emotion than I've seen in a long time from my Chameleon mentor.

But I nod shakily. "Okay." He's right. I'm doing this for more than just myself. I have to make it work.

"Let's worry about all that later. We need to get Mei inside." Seth's voice is unusually grim. He has a few phoenix flames over his body, and his eye is red instead of its usual hazel. The spell web flickers along his magic, dancing in time to it. He crouches down and picks me up off the ground like I don't weigh a thing.

In normal circumstances, I'd have a few things to say about being carried around like a child, but I can't quite manage to get them out. I really don't think I'm strong enough to walk on my own two legs just yet.

And I secretly like being held up against Seth's muscled chest. I have one arm around his neck, and the other rests against his body. Warmth flows into me through my hands, and my magic is dancing again, but for a different reason this time. Seth tightens his arms around me as if he can feel my reaction.

Si's expression becomes shuttered again, and he stares at us for a moment. I can see the indecision on his face, but I don't know what's causing it. My head is still too fuzzy to think my way through the possibilities. Then Si lets out an exasperated breath, and turns, striding back toward the Chameleon burrow. The entrance looks like something a hobbit might build, a large green-covered lump in the ground to one side of the training area. He lifts the green trap door, and we descend down into a long hallway lit by bulbs set into floor at regular intervals.

The Chameleons prefer to stay hidden, to tell no one where they live and to let very few outsiders in. It's a massive deal that they've allowed us to stay here.

The long passageway twists and turns until we reach the guarded front door. My body still feels like I've been dropped from the top of a cliff and then had a few elephants come by and trample over me. My vision is a little blurry, and I squint at the short, blond-haired guard by the door.

"Sir," he says, saluting Si.

Si nods, returns the salute, then presses his thumb to the coded lock.

The door slides open, and we're into the real living area of the Chameleon people. To the left of the door is another guard, this time with an array of closed-circuit cameras showing views around the outside and along the perimeter, as well as inside the passageway and around the other guard station.

There's muted bustle and activity in the long hall we're now entering. Thankfully, it's not too loud for my over-loaded senses. Chameleons don't like loud noise, or rush and hurry. They're calm, focused, and determined. They like to think. They like to decipher. They like to meditate. They like to look at every angle before they take action.

Oh, and they can fight like motherfuckers.

Fast, aggressive, and passionate. I don't know what comes over them when they fight, but I guess they never lose their cool, and they're still thinking as they kick each other's asses. I've watched several training matches since we arrived here, and it's always amazing. The skill, the level of training, the natural grace. No wonder the protectors I had were all Chameleons.

"Where to?" asks Si, looking at me.

I just blink up at him, not understanding.

"To our rooms," says Seth. "I think Mei needs rest."

"I'll grab some food and water and bring them to your rooms," Si says with a nod and disappears down a passageway to our right, where delicious smells indicate the kitchen is busy preparing lunch.

Seth tightens his grip on me fractionally, his eyes flashing with emotion, and strides through the middle of the hall. The guest rooms are not far from the hub, but far enough away to give us some privacy. Seth presses the security button by the entrance that's coded to our fingerprints, and the metal door slides open. I've been surprised by how high tech everything is here inside the Chameleon stronghold. For some reason, I always thought of Si as a low tech type of guy.

Never can tell I guess.

Seth strides into the room in our suite and carefully places me on the bed. I lean back into the pillows and close my eyes. My body still feels weak, battered, and sore like I've just been through a ten-hour training session with three hard-core fighters who were determined to beat me.

"How long did the attack last?" I ask, opening my eyes again.

"Less than a minute," says Seth from the bathroom. He emerges a second later holding a damp facecloth. He folds it and places it gently on my forehead. It's cool and soft, and the tension headache that I hadn't even noticed is soothed.

Seth's phone on the bedside table starts buzzing. He frowns over the screen. "It's my dad."

"You better answer it," I say, a croak catching my voice in the middle. Seth hasn't seen his father since he first became a phoenix. They're not exactly on good terms.

He shakes his head. "I can't deal with him right now."

"What if it's important? What if something has happened to your brother?" I don't know why I'm insisting. My head is pounding, my body aches. I should just fall asleep and let the world keep on happening. But some instinct inside me is burning, and I can't ignore it.

"He wants something from me. That's the only reason he'd bother calling." Seth's voice sounds so tired, it breaks my heart.

"Give him a chance. Maybe he just wants to check up on you?" Part of me is really hopeful. Why would my intuition be singing like this if it wasn't some kind of good news? I reach over and pick up the phone, handing it to Seth. He reluctantly takes it, and after a moment's hesitation, presses the button.

"Hey, Dad," he says, the caution in his voice saying volumes about his relationship with his father. "I'm good. How are you?"

Seth glances at me and then down at the lamp, like it's the most fascinating thing in the world. "No, I don't think that will be possible right now. There's too much—"

Seth stops, listening. I can hear the voice on the other end getting louder.

"I understand that but—"

The voice becomes even louder.

"You don't seem to understand—"

Seth tenses, and little flames appear around his neck, as the phoenix inside him rises to the surface again. His other self is so close at the moment, more so than I've ever seen him. I don't know if that's normal for a phoenix—maybe they just have fiery natures—or if it's something he's going to have to learn to control. The Seth I knew before his transformation was cool and controlled, a perfect example of a SIG agent. Should he be so different now?

Seth glances over at me and seems to calm down a fraction. He takes a breath, holds the phone away from his ear, the loud voice still jabbering in the background, and with some satisfaction presses the button to hang up.

I don't say a word, just wait for him to speak.

He doesn't. Just sits there, looking at nothing.

"What did he want?" I ask eventually.

Seth shakes his head and looks over at me. "He wanted me to come home. He feels there's information he needs to tell me."

"What if it's important?"

Seth shakes his head. "I don't care if it's important. He can't just call me and talk to me like that. I'm not a kid he can bully, not anymore."

4

The insistent buzzing of a phone wakes me. I blearily open my eyes and stare over at the bedside table. Seth's left his phone next to me. I reach over and look at the time on the screen. It's early evening, and it's his dad calling again.

I glance out toward the other room, but Seth doesn't seem to have heard the phone. Or perhaps he's ignoring it. Without thinking it through, I press the button.

"Hello?" I say.

"Who's this? Where's Seth?" The voice is gruff, and angry.

"This is Mei. I'm answering Seth's phone." I keep my voice calm. All the terrible pain from earlier has completely disappeared.

"I want to speak to Seth. Right now," he demands.

"You need to calm down," I say. "Or you'll never get to speak to him."

"Don't you tell me to calm down, young lady. You're the reason he's in this mess in the first place."

"How on earth do you figure that?" I ask, perplexed. I'm still half asleep.

"If he hadn't been on assignment guarding you, he would have been somewhere closer to home, and I would have been able to guide him through his change. None of this would have happened."

"None of what?" I ask, not following what he's talking about.

"I saw him on television. I saw the scar on his face, and the look in his eye. And he sided with *Vincent*."

I let out a breath. "Seth is fine. He had a bit of a rough start, but he's figuring it out."

"He needs to come home. There's information he needs to know about being a phoenix. What it means."

"I'll talk to him. See if I can get him to give you a call."

"See that you do." He hangs up on me, like he's a drill sergeant giving orders to a new recruit.

I hold the phone in my hand for a moment before replacing it carefully on the bedside table. I can see why his father rubs Seth the wrong way, but underneath the surly attitude, there was genuine concern.

I think back to the way Seth reacted when he was fighting Si. It was like he couldn't control his rage. It could have ended badly if I hadn't been attacked. Maybe there's something his father could tell him that would actually help.

Maybe we should go for a quick visit? Just to make sure. We could go and easily be back before my father arrives.

I pull back the covers and climb out of bed. I'm still wearing the shorts and T-shirt I changed into after we got back to the rooms, but I haven't eaten since breakfast, and my stomach growls. I must have missed Si with his provisions, but maybe there's a granola bar or something out in the living room.

I pad lightly into the living area and discover why Seth didn't hear anything. He's lying on the couch with his eyes shut and his headphones in. On the table there's the remnants of lunch, or maybe dinner. Bread, meats, and cheese. I butter myself a piece of bread and almost moan when I bite into it, the taste is so good. My stomach growls again, and Seth's eyes jerk open.

"Jeez, you gave me a heart attack!"

I give him a grin. "I can't help it if you were asleep on the job."

He ignores my comment. "Feeling better?" He sits up and pats the couch next to him.

I nod. "I feel like I've just woken for the first time in ten years." I sit down and cuddle in next to him, letting him curl his arm around me.

"You were sleeping like the dead in there," he says. "I couldn't have woken you if I'd tried."

"Did you talk to Si? Did he have any idea who it might have been?" I lean against his shoulder and breathe in his warm smoky scent.

"No. But he went to search the Chameleon archives, in case they had something useful for us."

I nod, enjoying the flavors of my bread and butter. Who knew it could be so good?

"What did it feel like?" asks Seth.

It takes a moment to remember what he's talking about; I'm so focused on the smooth taste of the butter. I pause in the middle of taking another bite. "Like I was being attacked in every direction by razor blades." I shiver at the memory. "Everything was too bright, too loud, too painful to touch. It was agonizing."

"And it felt like it was magic?"

"It had to have been. It was a direct attack on the spell web by someone with magic." Even saying the words out loud gives me goose bumps. The spell web inside me swirls and surges like an angry swarm of bees.

"Who would want to do that?" muses Seth. "Someone in Vincent's camp who is carrying on his work? Or a new enemy?"

"I don't know. It has to be a supernatural, because the humans have gone back to thinking we're figments of their imagination."

Seth shakes his head. "I would have said it was impossible for the humans to forget, except I witnessed it myself. The mass-hysteria induced hallucination angle your father designed worked like a charm."

"The power of the spell web," I say with a shrug.

"So what kind of supernatural might want to attack the spell web? Who would want to go back to the way we were?"

"Someone who hates other supernaturals? Someone who likes chaos?"

"Someone with the power to attack your mind," says Seth softly.

"We don't know anyone who has that power." Except... "What about the man in black? The guy you fought in the mountains? What were his powers?"

Seth shakes his head. "I have no idea if this is something he could do." He pauses, thinking. "What about Amos?"

I feel a pang in my chest. I'd forgotten about Amos—I don't even know where he is. What I do know is that I killed his father, and he's not going to be happy with me. The last time I saw him was when Carrick helped me escape from the Earthbound compound, and he was already a fair way to hating me at that point. I shrug helplessly. "He wasn't strong enough. Besides, I don't know how much he actually knew about what was going on. He didn't seem to know anything about it when Vincent was testing me the first time around."

"That could have changed." Seth hesitates. "He'll be angry at you, Mei. He was never entirely stable."

"Who is, these days?" I say, trying for lighthearted. It comes out sounding morose.

Seth's expression tells me just what he thinks about people who put themselves down. "We need to find a way to protect you from it, whatever it was. If someone is attacking you to get at the spell web, we need to find out how they're doing it, and how to stop it. If Si can't find anything here, we need to go see Carrick at the Earthbound compound. We could check the records there and ask Carrick to talk to the Mountain Super Elders. They're likely to know something."

I clear my throat. "There's one other place we should go first," I say.

"Where?"

"To see your dad."

Seth's expression closes down, and he immediately shakes his head. "No. I'm not going near him. Not until he learns how to play nice with others."

"I answered your phone," I say, knowing there's going to be an explosion.

"What?" Seth's eye darkens, flames flickering.

I can't help it; a shiver goes down my body. I love his phoenix side, even when it's raging. "It woke me up. I was disorientated."

"Please don't answer my phone again." He clearly wants to say more, but manages to hold it in. He clearly doesn't want to upset me, despite what I've just done.

But I can't back down. Seth might just need his dad's

help. "He sounded worried. Under the gruff, angry exterior, I mean. I don't think he knows how rude he's being."

"He's worried the wrong one of his sons got the phoenix blood."

"I know he expected it to be your brother. But maybe he just wants to help you now. He might have some information that will help you."

"Or he might just want to boss me around."

"You don't have to let him."

"You don't know my dad. He's always trying to be the dominant shifter in the room. It gets tiring."

"Are Ravens usually so dominant?" I don't know an awful lot about the Raven community. I do know they like to keep to themselves, kind of like the Chameleons. It's a wonder any of the shifter races ever meet.

"My father is a throwback. A Raven who wishes he was a phoenix."

I nod. It makes sense given what I know of his father. "Did you think you were a throwback too?"

Seth shakes his head. "I just thought I was a Raven whose shifter side didn't form properly. My father thought it was because I was the weaker son, but it turns out it was because I was a phoenix." Hurt vibrates through Seth's words. The spell web trembles, and I wish I could wrap my magic all around Seth and make his childhood suffering disappear.

"And your brother married Tracey in secret." I remember it now. "I bet your father was annoyed about that."

"Yeah, he didn't—"

A sharp knock reverberates on the door. I get up and open it, waving Si into our space.

"You feeling okay?" asks Si with more concern than I'm

used to from him. That worries me more than anything else that's happened so far today.

"I'm fine. The sleep did me good." I lead him back into the room and sit back down next to Seth, using his warmth to soothe me.

Si remains standing, pacing back and forth in front of us.

"Did you find anything more?" asks Seth, watching him pace like we're at a tennis match.

Si shakes his head. "There's mention of the Earthbound and their machines, but nothing about a power that could attack the spell web from a distance like that."

"We can't just let whatever it is attack her again," says Seth. "Who knows when the next attack will be, or what it will do to Mei." He tightens his grip on my shoulders, as if he can protect me by keeping me close.

"It didn't last long," I say hopefully. "Maybe it was a one-off?"

They both shake their heads without hesitation. There goes that thought.

"We need to get information. This is an unexpected complication. I thought we'd be safe here for a few weeks at least," says Si.

"Only a few weeks?" I say.

"The spell web is an important asset in the supernatural world. Before, it was always unquestioned that it was in the Earthbound's power. Now... well, let's just say that there are groups who see your ownership of the spell web as a more fluid concept, Mei."

Goose bumps rise up over my arms. "And you know this because...?"

"There are already groups forming on the dark web.

Talk in forums." Si shrugs. "We keep an eye on that sort of thing."

"So from now on, I'm going to have every crazy in Crazytown after me, 'cause they think I'm an easy mark?"

Si comes to a halt right in front of me. "It's our job to show them that you're not an easy mark. But for now, we have to be very careful. And information is our best ally. We need to know how they managed to get access into your mind, and we need to know it yesterday."

"How do we do that?"

"We need to go to the compound and talk to Elena and the other dragons. Talk to Carrick and the Mountain elders."

I glance at Seth and then back at Si. At least we're all on the same page about visiting Carrick. Except there's one other thing.... "And on the way we can stop and talk to Seth's father."

Beside me, Seth shakes his head. "No way. That's not part of our mission. You're the priority right now."

"No matter what's happened, your family has a lot more information than we do about phoenixes," I say, putting my hand on Seth's arm and leaning closer. "He might be able to help you with your ongoing... transition. And they might even have some useful information about *my* problem."

Seth stares at me, his hazel eye brooding. He won't deny me the chance to find out more about what might be attacking me, and the Ravens are such an old, tight-knit community, they really might know something useful. This isn't just about me interfering between him and his father. Much.

"Fine. But we're not staying long."

5

Soaring high above the small military town of Newport News, I let my wings flirt with the wind, the motion caressing my scales and soothing my soul.

A few weeks ago, I wouldn't have flown in so openly, but now that I'm the spell web, I can wrap it around us like a cloak and hide in plain sight.

Seth flies next to me, his fierce phoenix form giving off sparks as his massive fiery wings beat through the sky. Blood-red and golden flames undulate across his body, and his sharp eyes—strangely he doesn't carry his missing eye into his phoenix form—don't miss a thing on the ground below or in the sky around us. His long midnight-blue tail feathers oscillate out behind, and his large talons are curled at the ready.

Si is on my back, clutching tightly onto my back ridges. Si's never quite taken to flying with me, although to be fair, I did almost kill him when I was first learning.

Several times.

These days I'm much more practiced at being a dragon.

I dive down, taking the sweeping fall at a much easier angle than usual. I hear Si's strangled cry and feel him clutching tighter to my ridges. I give a huff of laughter and stretch my wings wider to catch the full rays of the sun.

Seth is leading the way, and it's not long before we're flying over the suburban area where Mike and Tracey live. Seth's father told us to meet him there.

Where should we land? I ask Seth.

Mike has a big backyard. You'll keep us hidden from prying eyes, right?

Right.

I turn and soar downward, following in Seth's wake.

The backyard is filled with kids' toys, including a trampoline and a big waterslide, but we manage to find a place to land. Si slides immediately to the ground and pulls out our clothes. I make the change and pull on the loose cotton pants and shirt I've borrowed from the Chameleons. They really understand the need for comfort and practicality.

I'm just putting on shoes when Mike appears at the door. Tracey's hovering behind him in the doorway, her sharp Eagle eyes taking everything in. The spell web glows powerfully over both of them. They're strong supernaturals in their own right. Just not as strong as a dragon and a phoenix.

I stand and walk over. They look nervous—and so they should. The last time we saw them, they called the SIG and turned us in.

"Seth," says Mike, holding out his hand. "Look I'm sorry—"

"Don't worry about it. You thought you were doing the right thing," says Seth, taking Mike's hand in a firm grip. His eye glows with suppressed fire.

Mike's eyes widen ever so slightly. "Dad's inside." He gestures behind him with his other hand.

Seth turns to Tracey. Last time, Tracey greeted him like he was her long-lost brother with a huge hug and admonitions. This time she looks less confident.

"Hey, Tracey." Seth leans in for a hug, and she puts her arms around him gratefully.

"We're both so sorry, Seth, we didn't understand—"

"Same goes, Tracey. You did what you thought was right. I'm not mad about it." Seth turns to me. "You remember Mei?"

I reach out with one hand and shake Mike's enormous fist. He tries to squeeze a little too tight, and I narrow my eyes and use some of my dragon strength right back at him.

He hastily pulls out of the handshake. I turn to Tracey and offer her my hand as well. She takes it hesitantly, her eyes still sharp, for all that she's repentant.

"Nice to meet you properly, Mei," she says.

I nod. "Nice to meet you both." Seth might have forgiven them, but as far as I'm concerned, they're still under warning for not looking out for him better.

Tracey can obviously see something in my expression that reflects my feelings, because she hastily steps back and motions for us to go into the house.

"Si's going to stay in the garden, keep an eye out just in case," I say as I walk past them. Si is loitering out the back looking serious and kind of scary.

The house is just as I remember it, even though last time I was in the middle of my transformation into a dragon and couldn't move to save myself. I follow Seth down the hall, through the kitchen, and into the living area. A rangy, solid-looking man with a crop of thick black hair is sitting on the couch, his arm across the back, drinking a beer. He's watching American football on television. The spell web glows powerfully over his body as well. The whole of Seth's family are very strong supernaturals. It's weird they thought Seth could possibly be so weak.

Seth's dad looks up as soon as we walk into the room, his brown eyes almost as sharp as Tracey's. "So you made it, did you?"

"We did." Seth stands at the door of the room, appearing relaxed, waiting for his father to do something. I'm standing close to him, so I feel the tension, but Seth hides it well.

I'm expecting his father to stand up and maybe shake our hands like Mike and Tracey, so I'm surprised when he continues to sit.

I see what Seth means about the dominance thing.

It's lucky I don't care about that kind of thing. "Are you going to stand up?" I say, my voice sharp. "Because if you really wanted to help Seth, that's what you'd do. You'd be polite. You'd make an effort."

His eyebrows arch up his forehead. "They told me you didn't speak much," he says. "Guess they got it wrong."

"Dad, this is Mei. Mei, this is my dad, Evan Barnes."

Evan slowly curls himself up and out of the couch. He's so tall that I have to crane my neck to catch his eyes. I hold out my hand, and he takes it in his. My hand is engulfed by his larger one, and he crushes it tightly. I narrow my eyes, trying to figure out if it's on purpose, or if he's just naturally strong.

It's lucky I had Jeff as a mentor. Thanks to him, I'm not easily intimidated or outmaneuvered by this kind of posturing. I give him grip for grip, just like I did with Mike.

I don't need to play the dominance game—but if I did, I'd win.

"Nice to meet you," I say, aiming for sweet and innocent.

His eyes narrow down on me, and I guess I didn't do a great job of it.

"So you're the dragon?" he says. "You don't look like much."

It's so rude, it's funny. I snort out a laugh, even as Seth tightens up next to me. I put one hand on his arm, letting him know I can handle it.

"We're here because you asked us to come. I convinced Seth to visit because I heard something in your voice that said this was important." I pause, watching him carefully. "But we could just as easily leave. We don't need you, and we don't need your attitude."

He stands there, as still as a mountain can stand, and then I see it. A whisper of fear. A suggestion that I was right.

There's something more going on here than any of us realized.

6

"I've been going over the family texts," says Evan.

We're sitting around the table in the kitchen, everyone with a coffee in front of them, courtesy of Mike and Tracey, who are both leaning against the kitchen counter. "The only time a phoenix is born into the Raven clan is when there's about to be some kind of major upheaval."

I nod. "That seems about right." I glance at Seth, and he's nodding.

"Only I don't think the upheaval we've gone through already is big enough."

"What do you mean?" It seemed pretty big to me.

Evan waves his hand dismissively. "I know you think you've had a major effect on the world, but it was over in a blip, in the context of hundreds of years. I think there's something more coming."

I watch him closely, using everything Jeff ever taught me about reading people. He seems too fidgety for a big guy. "What makes you think that?"

Evan glances at Mike and then at Seth. "The Raven clan

are tight. Outsiders are discouraged." He looks at Tracey and shrugs. "Sorry, girl, but it's true."

Tracey leans into Mike, who tightens his arm across her shoulders.

Evan continues: "But for all that we don't like outsiders, we keep a close watch. We're observers. We can see everything from a distance that gives us perspective that other supers lack."

"So what have you seen?" I don't know exactly where this is leading, but I'm not sure I like it.

"There have been a few incidents recently. Things that don't mean much on their own, but put together, they add up. It's like the smaller earthquakes that hint of the bigger one to come."

Seth is looking at his father with a puzzled expression. He has no idea what Evan's talking about either. "So Seth being born a phoenix, that's one of the signs you're talking about?"

"Yes."

"What else?" I feel like I'm squeezing blood from a stone.

"Demons." Evan says the word like it's the evilest thing in the world.

"Pardon?" I mean, I know they're not exactly great, but I'm pretty sure there's worse than demons. The man in black for one.

"There's a rising number of demons in the world. They're like a plague. Once they start to accumulate in numbers, it only gets worse, not better."

I frown over at Seth, then back at Evan. "How come I've never seen any evidence of this?"

"The SIG is keeping it quiet. Apparently they've got some expert working on it, who thinks he can harness the power of the demons for their energy."

I hesitate, wanting to know how Evan knows about the internal workings at the SIG. I manage to not ask the question. "Is that possible?" I ask instead, thinking of the demon I set free at SIG headquarters. I bet that demon wouldn't have been happy about being used as energy.

"I don't know. My sources couldn't confirm it. But I do know that messing around with demons is a dangerous business. Especially since the last chalice died more than twenty years ago."

"Chalice?" I repeat the word stupidly. I've never heard of a chalice, and I've been tutored by the best.

Evan waves one hand. "A chalice can call, control, and kill demons. They're the ones who keep the balance steady. The last of 'em was killed off. Without a chalice and with a rise in the numbers of demons..." Evan shakes his head. "I think we're about to experience something much worse than a few humans getting scared."

Part of me wants to stand up and tell him the things that happened with the Earthbound and the humans was about far more than a few humans getting scared. But if he's right about the expanding demon population, he could also be right that this is a much bigger threat.

Dammit.

"How does Seth fit into this?"

"A phoenix isn't as affected by demons as other supers. They have some limited ability to work with them. But a phoenix is often more of a warning sign than a weapon we can use against what's about to happen."

"Have you heard any rumors?" I ask Seth.

He shakes his head. "No. But I think it's definitely time to check in with your father. He might know something. Can we meet him at the Earthbound compound?"

I nod in agreement, and turn back to Evan. "So what are

the Ravens doing about all this?"

He blinks, and then stares at me like I'm a weird insect under a microscope. "Ravens are just the observers."

"Well, do you personally have any ideas?" He's so keen to be dominant, let him do some of the thinking.

"We need to find out what the exact demon numbers are. Find out if the rumors are actually true."

I nod, thinking it through. "Who would be able to do that?"

"I have a few resources. A supernatural consultant or two I could approach," says Evan carefully, like he's trying to protect his sources from me.

Like I care. "Do the Ravens have records? Maybe more information about demons that we could access?"

"We do. But only Ravens are allowed to read them." Evan's voice takes on a hint of superiority again.

"Do you want us to do something about the demons? Or should we just leave it up to the Ravens?" I ask, glaring at him. This guy is such a jerk. I squeeze Seth's hand under the table, trying to keep myself calm.

"Am I still considered part of the Raven clan?" asks Seth quietly, before his father can answer my rhetorical question.

Evan scowls at Seth like he's an idiot. "Of course you are."

"Then perhaps you could take me to the clan records, and we could search them? I'd like to know as much as I can about being a phoenix as well."

Evan nods. "There's information about your abilities that will help you."

I sit there, tapping my finger on the wooden table. Could the attack on me have been anything to do with the demon plague? Could it be the *demons* finding a way into my head, where other supers can't go? I shiver. I hope not.

"I think this is important enough that I should stay here with Dad," says Seth, his tone reluctant. "Maybe I could meet you at the Earthbound compound in a couple of days?"

Every instinct inside me is screaming *no*, that we need to stay together. But I'm pretty sure it's just the part of me that's scared of losing Seth again. "We do need to know more. About *all* our problems," I say carefully. I squeeze his hand under the table again, and he returns it with a tight grip.

Evans sharp eyes swivel to me. "You've got other problems?"

I sigh, my gaze still on Seth. Can I trust his family? I have my doubts, but Seth nods imperceptibly. He thinks we can.

I turn back to Evan. He's large and muscled, and yet still somehow manages to even look like a Raven. His nose is beaky, his hair Raven black, just like Seth's. His intelligent eyes are trained on my face, not missing a single thing.

"I was attacked yesterday. Something invaded my body and tried to attack not only me, but the spell web. It was trying to destroy it. We need to know what has the power to do that, and how to stop it."

Evan sits back in his chair, his breath releasing in one shocked sound. "That's a big problem. I'm not sure if we could deal with it being broken again."

"We dealt with it before," I say. "It wouldn't be ideal, but not the end of the world."

"We didn't have a demon plague about to be let loose last time."

I lean forward, studying his face. "Is that what's going to happen?"

"Yes. And if we don't have the spell web to protect us from the humans, we're fucked."

7

Seth's arms wrap around me, and I put my cheek against his chest, taking solace in his radiating warmth.

"You'll take care of yourself?" he asks.

"You'll be a couple of days behind me. It'll be fine." But I don't move from the circle of his arms.

"I wouldn't stay here unless I thought it was absolutely necessary." He puts his chin on my head, holding me even closer. His heart beats against my cheek.

"I know," I say, swallowing down the petulant part of me that wants to keep Seth with me. "And I agree that you should stay here. We need all the information we can get. I'll be fine at the Earthbound compound."

"You be careful, okay?" he says, leaning back, and catching my gaze. "No going off to save anyone. You're much more of a target now. You were never precisely under the radar, but now everyone knows who you are."

I shrug. "Only the supers."

"That's enough. Not everyone agrees with the spell web

being back in place. And remember what Si said about groups wanting to take control of the spell web."

"I know. I'll be careful."

Seth pulls back completely, and I reluctantly let him go. He leans down and places his lips over mine in a fleeting kiss that's not nearly enough. Heat flares between us, and I put my hands up to his face, deepening the kiss, hungry for more. Seth's arms go back around me, and suddenly we're kissing like we're never going to see each other again.

A throat clears behind us. "You better go, if you're going to avoid the human rush hour," says Evan. He seems perfectly neutral on the surface, but I catch an undertone of animosity. Is it because I'm not a Raven?

Or something else?

I pull away. Seth's eyes are filled with regret, and I know he wishes he wasn't staying here with his father.

"It's important," I whisper into his ear. "And only for a couple of days."

He nods. "He's right. You better get going."

Si's already waiting for me in the backyard. I undress behind a shed and make the change into my dragon form.

I gaze one more time toward Seth standing on the back step next to his father. It's only for a few days, I remind myself as Si climbs on my back.

Evan shuffles next to Seth, and my whole attention is caught by his movement. He looks shifty, like he's trying to hide something. Why didn't I notice that before?

Tell your father that if anything happens to you, I will come back with a dragon army and destroy the Ravens. Completely and without mercy.

The words flow out of me into Seth's head based on some instinct I can't explain.

His eyes widen in surprise.

I nod my head at him, gesturing toward his father.

Seth reluctantly turns to his father, and I wait while he repeats what I've just said. Evan steps back, his gaze snapping to mine. He looks afraid.

He should be. I could take on a Raven in my sleep. Seth is mine, and I won't lose him. I growl and huff out smoke, posturing so it's directly aimed at Evan.

Watch out for your father, I say to Seth. *I don't trust him.*

Neither do I, Seth answers immediately. *Take care of yourself.*

You too.

Snapping out my wings, I leap into the air.

Si clings to my back, so I can't do the aerobatics I'm desperate to do to clear my head. Something feels off about the Ravens and their warning. It's only because I know Seth can take care of himself that I feel okay about leaving him there. That, and I think his brother and Tracey will look out for Seth this time. They seemed genuinely regretful about their actions.

It's his father I don't trust.

The feeling is so strong, I almost turn around and head back right then and there.

But the wind picks up my wings, and as the cooling air spreads across my body, I start to think clearly again. We need information, on everything. The demons. Seth's changes as a phoenix. Whatever is attacking me.

And the Ravens are the observers. The watchers. If anyone is going to have some useful information, it's them. Seth knows what he's doing. He's smart. Savvy. It's going to be fine.

So I keep flying.

It's a couple of hours by dragon wing to the compound. I have to remember to stay lower in the sky for Si's sake—I almost killed him when I first changed because I went too high—and I try to stay away from inhabited areas.

Not because the humans would see me or know what I was. More as a habit that feels safer.

When I finally land at the compound, the day has properly begun. The heat of the sun is pounding down on the desert oasis, and it feels like we've been up for hours.

Si slides down the side of my flank and stumbles as he lands, his usual grace missing. I'm immediately contrite and wish I'd taken a rest stop for him. I always forget that it's a difficult journey for the person on my back. Not everyone is as strong as I am in the air.

Guards come striding out to meet us, and my magic surges with remembered fear and rage. I rear up onto my back legs, fire forming in my belly in preparation for meeting the enemy. It's only when I recognize the insignia of the Mountain supers that my instinctive reaction simmers down. I don't relax completely, though—they killed Liling after all—until I see Carrick's enormous shape in the background.

"Mei! It's good to see you," he booms up at me. "To what do I owe this pleasure?"

Si strides up to him and holds out his hand. "She'd probably like somewhere to change into human form," he says by way of greeting as the two shake hands.

Carrick gestures up to the roof. "Head that way, there's a spot set up, along with clothes to change into." He squints up into the sky as if waiting for something. "No Seth?"

"We left him with his family for a couple of days," says Si. "They've alerted us to a possible problem, so he's stayed behind to look into it."

Carrick nods, as if this is only to be expected. I'm desperate to ask him what he's thinking but can't do it in this form. So I nod down at them both and take off toward the roof.

By the time Carrick and Si open the door to the roof, I'm back in human form, and wearing the loose-fitting pants and tank top I found in the locker. It's typical of Carrick to think of everything.

I walk over and give him a huge hug. He's saved me more than once. I'm hoping he's going to be able to do it again.

"It's good to see you," I say.

"I'm glad you've come visiting," he says with a grin, his large craggy face showing real pleasure.

I take a moment to soak up the feeling of being welcomed. It's not something I feel much of these days. Suspicion and outright animosity seem to be more usual. Magic from the spell web inside me rises up and curls around us of its own accord. There's something about Carrick and his Mountain magic that has always connected with my dragon powers. Apparently the spell web feels the same about him.

"Come, come inside. Let's get you something to eat and drink before we talk more about our problems."

I give him a sharp look. He's got problems as well? Is there nothing that's working as it should? But I nod and acquiesce to his suggestion. Si looks dead on his feet, and it makes me wonder if he even slept last night. Knowing him, he probably kept watch all night, just to make sure we were okay.

As we tramp inside, leaving the bright sunshine outside, a shiver tingles across my skin. I'm back in the Earthbound compound again, and it doesn't feel any better now than it did the last time.

———————

8

"So the Ravens think there's a demon plague?" says
Carrick, doubt in every line of his body. We're in a
small room near the main hall, seated in large
padded chairs more suited to Carrick's bulk than my smaller
frame. Si is standing near the window, looking out, as
Carrick and I exchange news and drink lemonade.

"You don't think it's possible?" I ask, curious about his
immediate animosity at the mention of the Ravens.

Carrick shrugs. "They're not exactly reliable witnesses.
They're proud and argumentative. Stubborn as hell. They've
fallen out with every other race of shifters. Practically every
other super race there is."

"Why?" I ask, leaning forward. I don't understand how
Seth can be so normal, and everyone else in his family—
apparently everyone who's a Raven—is an asshole.

"They're a closed group. They have their own set of
rules."

I frown, not quite understanding whatever it is that he's
hinting at. "How did they manage to raise someone like
Seth?"

"I have a feeling he was an outcast," says Carrick slowly. "Did you say his father didn't really pay much attention to him? Thought he was weak growing up?"

I nod.

"There's a chance he was kept out of the real inner circle. And his brother married an Eagle?"

I nod again.

"That would've hurt his father's standing in the community. He'll be itching to get himself back up the hierarchy."

"Why would he demand that Seth come back now?"

"Are you kidding? Seth's a phoenix. The strongest male line there is, according to the Ravens."

I think back to Evan's shifty appearance as I left. "He won't try to hurt Seth, will he?"

"Never. Seth is his key to recognition within the Raven hierarchy. But...."

"But what?" I ask impatiently.

Carrick is smirking as he looks down at me. "He might try to marry Seth off."

"What?" Surprise makes me squeak out the word.

Carrick grins. "I'm sure Seth won't let it happen. But it's a great way to cement the power of a phoenix. To marry a high-ranking Raven girl."

My gut clenches. I thought I'd lost Seth not so long ago. I'm not going to let him marry some other girl. "Seth wouldn't do that."

Si turns from the window. "What if he has no other choice? What if it's for the betterment of the supernatural community?" he asks, his voice neutral. It reminds me of the way Jeff used to ask questions.

I glare over at him. "Is that the case? Is that what you think?"

"What if it was? Could you make that kind of a decision?"

I take a breath, and then another. I've been forced to do many things in my lifetime. I've had to make decisions for the wider community, rather than myself. But give up Seth? I shake my head. "That's not the situation. I don't have to give up Seth."

Si stares at me a moment longer and then shrugs and looks back out the window.

I feel like I've failed some kind of test. But I can't help it, I've had to give up too much. A normal life. Friends. Family. I'm not giving up Seth.

"I'm sure Seth wouldn't marry anyone...." Carrick grins. "At least not without telling you first."

I glare at Carrick, even knowing he's teasing me, and is enjoying my discomfort. It's like having a really big, really annoying older brother. "How's Elena?" I ask, trying to divert attention away from me.

Carrick's face darkens. "She's just like the Ravens. Argumentative and thinks she knows everything better than anyone else."

His answer surprises a laugh out of me. "It's going that well?"

"Worse."

My gaze sharpens on Carrick. "You're not having problems maintaining this place? We wouldn't want to lose it to anyone else."

Carrick shakes his head. "No, it's fine. She's just a pain to deal with. Nothing I can't handle."

"Is that the problem you were referring to earlier?"

"Part of it. The other part is that we're having trouble deciphering the Earthbound texts. It's in some kind of weird language that we're struggling to understand."

"I thought Elena knew their language?"

Carrick shrugs. "So did she."

I lean back in the chair, a huff of breath knocked out of my chest. Those texts are why I'm here. If no one can read them…. "Can I have a look at them?"

"Sure. No harm in looking."

We stand, and Carrick gestures for me and Si to follow him through the door. He leads us to a stairwell and down a series of stairs until we're deep in the bowels of the building. Not quite the dungeon levels that I'm familiar with, but at least three stories down into the ground.

It feels… enclosed down here. Like the earth is holding us in its hands. The protection of the Mountain supers has given it a warm feeling that was never here before. I glance at Si to see if he feels it too, but he's just as impossible to read as usual.

I let out a breath that I didn't know I was holding and relax a little more. Vincent is dead. I don't have to worry about some new and terrible torture around every corner. I'm not here to rescue someone. There are no machines set to steal my magic.

Carrick opens a door leading out of the stairwell and into a long corridor. All along the halls are wooden doors set back into the stone, each with strange numbers and letters carved into the doors.

"This is the library level," he says, gesturing at the doors. "Each of these rooms has thousands of books, on all possible topics."

I slow down so I can touch the letters carved into the doors. They're not in any language I can understand, but they look beautiful, like poetry. My fingers graze the carvings, the hard wood cool to the touch.

The double doors Carrick stops at are larger than the

rest, made of a dark wood, ornately carved with men and women dressed in the robes worn by the Earthbound of old.

They're carrying knives, stones, and bows and arrows, and they all have angry expressions. They're probably off to kill a dragon or two. The thought sends a shiver through me. For all that Carrick's presence has made this place safer for me, I have to remember what the Earthbound represent, what they did to people like me.

I can't relax around here.

And it's too dangerous to forget.

C arrick puts a key into the large metal lock and pushes open the doors, revealing a large library inside. The books are old, leather-bound tomes for the most part sitting on large shelves, almost to the top of the room. I take a sniff, expecting the room to be musty or damp, but it's dry and just smells of old books.

"It's protected by a state-of-the-art air filtration system. The Earthbound were paranoid about their books," says Carrick, clearly able to read my expression.

"Have you been able to decipher any of them?" I ask. I'm pretty sure they're filled with fun ways to kill dragons. It's been the focus of the Earthbound's existence for the last three hundred years. Why stop now?

So much energy and innovation put into the art of killing dragons. Of killing people like me.

I shiver again.

"Some. But none of the ones we can understand have the information we need." Carrick glares off to one corner of the room. "It's proving harder than expected." He leads us in the direction he's glaring, and Si and I follow him. As we walk down between two rows of books, I reach out and run my fingers along the leather bindings. The ancient leather is hard under my fingertips.

When Elena comes into view with two other women, all dressed in long robes, I realize why Carrick was frowning. His whole body is bristling, and the tension in the room goes up a few notches.

I struggle to keep the grin off my face as I watch Carrick and Elena glare at each other. The spell web flickers in response to the electricity that's sparking between them. They might dislike each other on the surface, but there's chemistry between them that's stronger than any difference of opinion.

"Elena, you remember Mei?" says Carrick, in a formal voice I've never heard him use before.

Elena glares at him. "I haven't sustained a knock to the head since I saw her last. Of course I remember Mei." She turns her gaze to me, and I feel the full force of her personality through her jewel-like eyes. She's a dragon, another of my kind. But she's a priestess, one of a select few who chose to work with the Earthbound to help them cage and destroy the dragons of old.

It's hard not to feel animosity toward her. The death of all those dragons can be laid partially at her feet.

Except she helped me defeat Vincent. She almost died because of the very machines the original priestesses helped create.

"It is good to see you, Mei. I'm pleased you've come to visit."

"Hi, Elena." I walk closer and lean over the book she has open on the table in front of her. My eyes sweep the page, some part of me hoping that maybe I'll magically be able to read it. I can't. "Carrick says you're having trouble deciphering the books?"

She scowls down at the book in front of her as if it's the book's fault. "It's written in a slightly different dialect than we remember." She nods to the other two women. "This is Susan and Melody. They are priestesses like me."

I nod at them both, noticing their slightly cooler expressions. They both seem... reluctant. I glance over at Carrick and wonder if he realizes their feelings, or if they're keeping it too well hidden. A conversation for later.

"Why do you think it's in a different dialect?" asks Si, moving in and leaning over another of the open books. His expression is closed, and I can't tell if he can read it any more than I can.

"Some of these texts seem newer. Like they rewrote the older ones and made up a new language to keep their secrets close." Elena shrugs one elegant shoulder. "Perhaps to prevent this very situation, dragons like us coming through and deciphering their mysteries."

"So these texts are indecipherable?" I say. Disappointment ricochets around in my chest. How am I going to find out who and what is attacking me?

A shuffling sound carries across the silent room, and moments later an old man hobbles into view from the side of the nearest shelf. He's old and craggy, the lines on his face as deep as a rock cavern. He's small but seems to take up more space than he should. I recognize him immediately—Carrick's grandfather, the old Mountain super who performed Tarsal's funeral and lambasted me at the same time.

He hates me.

I swallow hard, trying to keep myself steady in the face of the onslaught I'm sure is about to come my way.

"Grandfather," says Carrick, his voice warming up. "I didn't know you were still here."

His grandfather looks up from under bushy eyebrows, his eyes still sharp. "Where else would I go, lad?" His voice is low and gravelly, and the spell web curls around him, almost like it's holding him up. He turns his gaze to me. This time, there's none of the condemnation.

There's not a lot of appreciation either.

"So you're back. To cause more problems, no doubt."

"I'm trying to *solve* our problems," I say, without thinking.

"Really? Is that what you call it?" You could cut glass with the sarcasm in his voice.

"Grandfather, leave her be," says Carrick in a long-suffering tone.

I clear my throat. "Well, I'm no help with understanding this stuff. It just looks like strange markings to me."

Si nods his head in agreement. "Perhaps we need to search for others who have the lost language in their arsenal?"

I glance at him, pretty sure his sharp eyes caught the lack of enthusiasm from the two other priestesses.

Elena stands quickly. "We're in the process of decoding the language. It is close to the old one. We feel we will understand it very soon. Within weeks."

Weeks? "What if we don't have that long?" I ask. I could be attacked at any moment. Weeks seems an unbearable amount of time to suffer with that hanging over my head.

Elena turns to me, her eyes wide. "What is happening? Why the rush?"

I shake my head. "We just need the information in these texts as soon as possible. We don't have weeks." *I* might not have weeks, but I'm not going to tell her that.

"We're already working all hours of the day," says one of the other priestesses sharply. Susan I think. Her hands are curled tightly on the book in front of her.

Carrick raises his hands in a placating manner. "We will continue to work all the hours we can. But we can't just magic up the ability to speak this language, Mei. We have to decipher it."

"There are some that could magic it up," says Carrick's grandfather darkly, his expression grim.

My ears perk up. "Who?"

"No one we'd want to deal with," says Carrick, his voice equally grim.

"Who?" I ask again. Dread fills my stomach.

"You know him as the man in black."

It's a punch to the gut. The supernatural who convinced the Mountain King to attack me? The man who killed Liling? Who fought Seth in midair?

There's no way I would ever ask for his help.

Deciphering these books and finding a way to figure out who is attacking me seems even further away than before.

10

"His kind are the secret keepers. They can decode, decipher, figure out anything they set their mind to," says Carrick's grandfather, not giving up on the Man in Black so easily.

"He's called a Minokawa?" I ask, my heart sinking into my stomach. He killed Liling without even blinking. It didn't matter that he was aiming for me.

"Yes. Almost as unique as a dragon in this day and age."

"And he could figure out this language?" I gesture at the books out on the table, open to the indecipherable information inside them. Frustration builds inside me at how close we are to finding things out, and yet how impossible it is to get it.

"In minutes," says Carrick. "The only problem is what he'd do with the information. And whether he'd feel inclined to pass it on to us."

"His kind are almost as ancient as the dragons," adds Carrick's grandfather. "They hate dragons, for some ancient reason known only to them."

"He was a black lizard, in the sky, when he fought Seth,"

I say, remembering the fear as I watched from the ledge below, unable to help.

He nods. "They're a mix of dragon and bird. In their Minokawa form, they have a beak and claws of steel, eyes so black they're like mirrors into your soul, and feathers that can be used as knives, they're so sharp."

"Is that all true?" I ask, turning to Carrick. "It sounds like a fairy tale used to scare children."

Carrick shrugs. "They're powerful, that much I know. The man in black had the Mountain King in his thrall, although we didn't know how much until the revolution. We had no idea of his real plans." His eyes are pools of sadness. He carried Liling's bloodied body for me, found a healer to tell me exactly what he already knew. Liling was dead.

Because of me.

"The old King's daughter was killed by a gang of humans," I say, swallowing down the lump that is forming in my throat. Suddenly all I can see is Liling's bloodied face.

"He was grief-stricken," agrees Carrick. "More susceptible perhaps."

My magic swirls up around me, agitated by my memories of Liling's last moments. Dragon fire builds in my belly, even though I'm in the wrong shape to throw it out. I try to stay calm, to keep my thoughts—and thereby my magic—under control, but the painful feeling moves from my gut and radiates out. Even the spell web is rolling up and down inside me like a choppy sea expecting a storm.

"So we should approach this man?" asks one of the priestesses, oblivious to the undercurrents.

"No," I say, shaking my head. "We will not." I clench my fists, trying to fight the terrible feelings swirling through my body. I see the man in black's soulless eyes as he shot at me, his frustration when he realized his bullet hit Liling instead.

The memory of her face as she died. The blood, the fear. Fire burns inside me, wanting to get out. My magic churns, pushing at my insides, making me gag. It's so powerful, overwhelming. It feels like my burning dragon magic is about to erupt out of me like a beach ball being held under the water. I don't know how I got to this point so quickly, to the edge of reason. My hands are shaking, and I glance over at Si, but he seems oblivious to my reaction. The only thing I can think of to control my reaction is to use the spell web. I clutch at the comforting presence of it, drawing it out, and allow it to coat my magic like maple syrup over pancakes.

For a moment it works, and it feels like I've just added ice cream to those imaginary pancakes. A breath of cool air blows through the fire inside me.

And then it gets worse.

Tiny pinpricks of pain roll over me, attacking from every direction. The pain becomes so agonizing. I let out a groan, and lean forward over the table, balancing myself on my arms. Numbness crawls up my legs, unbearable in its absence of feeling. My legs are like jelly. I'm on fire with the excruciating pain of the memories inside me. My whole body is throbbing, enflamed, tormented.

"Mei? What's the matter?" Carrick's voice breaks through the agony.

"It's another attack," says Si from behind him. "This is the second time. Someone is attacking the spell web through her."

His words open a crack of light inside me. This isn't my emotions taking over, the physical manifestation of pain from Liling's death. It's not my erratic magic getting out of control. It's not even the spell web doing something strange.

This is another attack.

When I look closely at it, I realize it's the same pain as

last time. The fire ants are back with their pincers and their little glass knives, pounding into my flesh. The bears are there, clawing into my skin. Fear crawls its way up my body, dragging dread and shuddering apprehension in its wake. I can't help it. I squeeze my eyes shut and scream in pain. My body collapses, and it feels like I've folded in on myself, like a black hole collapsing.

Hands grasp me on either arm and lower me to the floor. I don't know which way is up. I can't feel anything except the heat of hands on my arms. It's the only thing that keeps me sane.

"Mei, you must concentrate. Push the pain away, push the attackers away. Build a wall, brick by brick around you. They cannot harm you here." Si's smooth voice penetrates the wall of pain.

"I can't...." Pain. Pain. Pain.

"Mei, you must. Concentrate. Use the spell web." Si's voice sounds as close to panicked as I've ever heard him.

I close my eyes and focus inside me. I try to use the spell web again; it's elusive, hidden through a cloud of fog that I can't quite access. The only thing it achieves is that the pain intensifies. I can't tell where my attackers are coming from. Or on which front to fight them. They're invisible. All-powerful.

I moan as another wave of pain suffocates my body.

"Mei," interrupts another voice sharply. "Listen to me. You must *stop* using the spell web. Hide it away inside you."

I frown in confusion. "How?" I manage to pant out the word.

"Imagine you're closing it up in a little box. Put the lid on tightly."

I squeeze my eyes shut, concentrating on picturing a little box. The spell web is dancing inside me, moving too quickly for me to touch it. The fog inside me has intensified, making everything seem vague and difficult. Magic tingles along my nerve endings, and I try to grab the spell web. It skips away from me, out of reach.

I moan, unable to control my reaction as more painful pin pricks devour my skin.

"Come on, Mei, try harder," says the same voice.

I gasp in a breath and grab at the spell web again. This time, it falls into my hands, bucking and rocking as it tries to get free. I don't understand why it's so important, but I do as the stern voice says. I take the little box I've imagined and push the spell web down inside it. The agonizing needles in my flesh let up slightly. I keep going until nothing is visible, and I can slam the lid over it.

I take a breath. And then another. The pain subsides, sliding away.

Opening my eyes, I gaze up into the lined face of Carrick's grandfather. His eyes are sharp, focused on me.

"Am I okay?" I ask, my voice less than a whisper.

"You're in more trouble than you realize," he says gruffly.

11

Carrick hands me a drink, and I take a sip, wincing when I taste whiskey.

"Really?" I ask, coughing as it burns down my throat.

"It woke you up, didn't it?" he says mildly.

I'm sitting in one of the enormous chairs back in Carrick's private room. I was still dazed as he carried me here, with Si and his grandfather trailing in our wake.

They're all standing in front of me, staring down at my face like I'm some kind of strange bug they have to figure out.

"What did he mean 'I'm in more trouble than I realize'?" I ask Carrick, my voice croaky. I'm not feeling entirely confident about the answer his grandfather is going to give me.

Carrick's grandfather steps up, his bushy eyebrows waggling like they've got a mind of their own. "I'll answer that for myself, if you don't mind," he says sternly. Then he hesitates, an action so uncharacteristic it fills me with dread like nothing else would have.

I blink, trying to focus on his face, to see what no one else can see, to understand the lines and wrinkles, to figure out the glint in his eyes. But I can't do it. I can no more see what he's about to tell me than I can tell the future.

"You're not being attacked by some external force," he says.

"But—"

He holds up his hand for silence. I bite my lip.

"It's not from an outside source. It's the spell web itself attacking you."

All the air leaves my body in a whoosh. I shake my head. "No. That's not true. I can feel it. I *know* it's not the spell web attacking me."

He looks down at me in an almost kindly way. That by itself is enough to make me believe what he's saying. He's not the kindly type. "It's not on purpose. It's just the nature of the spell web."

"Why would it be attacking me? *I'm* the spell web. It's *part* of me." I feel like a whining kid, but I don't understand what he's saying.

"That's why the original Earthbound group created the spell web globe. They tried to host it in a single supernatural, even a dozen. But it never worked. They were never strong enough. The spell web always ate them up, piece by piece, until they died painful and agonizing deaths."

The image makes me shudder. "That's a cheery way to tell me about it," I mutter. Thoughts swirl in my head as I try to understand what he's telling me.

"Grandfather, are you sure of this?" asks Carrick, his expression cautious. "Where are you getting your information?"

The old man waves one hand at Carrick. "It's one of the

old stories. Passed to me by my grandfather. I thought perhaps because she's a dragon she could hold it." His eyes turn sad. "But perhaps not."

"But it worked, what you had me do," I say. "The concentrating thing." The spell web wouldn't devour me. Surely it can't be true?

"It will work for a time. You are powerful. You can stave off the inevitable for a while. But the spell web is enormous, volatile, corrosive. It will devour you in the end."

"How long?" asks Si sharply.

"Till it consumes her?" He shakes his head. "I don't know. I just know that these are no external attacks. It's the spell web itself, and it won't stop until it has every drop of her power consumed."

"And then what?" I ask.

"You will die. And when you die, so will the spell web. The humans will see us again, and there'll be repercussions through the whole of the supernatural community."

"But... there must be another way—"

"My grandfather was clear on it. The only way to hold the spell web is in a globe like the one the Earthbound built, and you destroyed. That globe was unique, it took years to create and build."

I shake my head. "All those books in the library. There must be more information inside them. Once we figure out the language, we'll know more," I say desperately.

"You may not have weeks."

I stare at him, stunned. "How long do I have?"

"I don't know. But that attack seemed brutal."

"Are you sure we can't make another globe?"

"We don't know how. And even if we did, we don't have enough time. I'm sorry, Mei."

He truly does look sorry. He's basically just announced my death sentence. At least he's got the grace to look sad about it.

"And what happens when I die? And the spell web is destroyed?"

"We'll go back to how it was before, when the humans could see us. Except this time, there will be no dragon shifter who knows the spell web like you do to save us all."

I swallow hard. This is bad news. Not just bad news, the *worst* news. For everyone. My chest constricts, and I have trouble taking another breath. I can't see a way out, or a path forward that's going to save me. Black dots appear in my vision and I blink, trying to clear them away.

Si steps forward. "This is not definitive. We have other options to look into, Mei. We don't have to give up based on a fairy story."

Carrick's grandfather huffs out an offended breath. "My people are also record keepers. We do not lie, we do not exaggerate, and we do not tell *fairy stories.*"

"You might not *think* you're lying, but I prefer to get my information from sources more solid than a story told to you by your grandfather when you were a child." Si's hiding it well, but he's just as affected by this news as I am. The knowledge gives me comfort, despite the thoughts raging inside me.

"I have perfect recall—"

"Enough," says Carrick, motioning sharply with his hand. "Thank you, Grandfather, this is important information. We will certainly be able to act upon it. But—" He glares at Si when he tries to interrupt again. "—we won't use it as an excuse to give up on Mei, or to find an alternative option."

I look gratefully over at Carrick, finding solace in his solid form, and his calm acceptance of the disaster his grandfather has just described. It's only when I notice the tiny tic at the corner of his eye that I realize he has no more idea than I do what the hell we're going to do.

12

"I'll be there as soon as I can," says Seth. His voice is tight, stressed.

I hold the phone tighter against my ear. The colorful flowers of the garden I'm standing in seem out of place. I haven't been able to tell him what Carrick's grandfather said yet. He sounds like he's going through a whole lot where he is too. I don't want to add to his stress levels just yet.

Maybe it'll be easier to tell him in person.

"You need to look up anything to do with the spell web," I say instead, trying to keep my voice from wobbling. It doesn't work. Seth doesn't seem to notice, which says a lot about how distracted he is at his end. "And the globe they used to have."

"The globe?" he asks absently. There are voices in the background, talking at him. "Okay, okay," he says, clearly not to me. "Look, Mei, I'm sorry, I have to go. There's some big ceremony they want me to be a part of. I'll call you back as soon as it's over, and we can talk more. Don't do anything crazy without me."

"Okay," I say. "I'll—" But he's already hung up.

I drop my hand into my lap and sit there staring down at my phone. I hope Seth's okay. He sounded like he was stretched to the breaking point, with nowhere else to go. It makes me want to transform and just fly to him, to comfort him, and protect him. I think of his father, eagerly using his previously unwanted son as leverage for more power. I hope Seth can withstand his father's machinations.

The urge to protect Seth is so strong, I take a couple of steps in the direction of the lawns. But what if it's me that I have to protect him from? What will he do when he finds out the spell web is going to devour me piece by piece? My chest heaves. That's pain I can't save either of us from.

I sit down on the bench seat in the tiny back garden of the compound where I'm hiding out. The others keep giving me sad glances, and it's driving me nuts. It feels like they've all given up on me, even though they're saying we're going to fight and find a way out.

The crunching of footsteps on the stone path makes me look up.

Damien Walker, ex-SIG agent and master spy, is walking toward me, his face inscrutable. He looks like an ordinary guy, brown hair, brown eyes, average build. That's why he gets overlooked, and it's exactly why he's so dangerous. He's also my father, the other half of my dragon heritage.

I've been expecting him. I'm sure Carrick has given him the update on my attacks. I stare at him, waiting to see what kind of platitudes he might have come to offer. At least he's not giving me the same sad eyes as the others.

"Hi, Dad," I say, standing up. My legs feel heavy, but I manage to stay upright.

He walks up to me, and closer in, I can see how pale he is, the extra lines around his eyes that he never used to have. He only just changed into his Chameleon form for the first time with my help, and I wonder if it's causing him problems. "How're you doing?" I want to ask if he's changed into a Chameleon again, but I can't quite manage it. Somehow it feels too personal.

"I hear you're getting yourself into trouble again?" He says the words softly, like he doesn't want to disturb the bees in the flowers next to us. And he completely ignores my question.

I let out a small sigh. "Aren't I always?"

"Jeff used to complain to me about how much of a fire-cracker you were. I should have known then what he was hinting at. I just thought he meant you were a pain in the butt."

"Same thing, maybe?" I say with the ghost of a smile.

"Perhaps." He opens his arms wide, and I lean in for a hug. It's not as comfortable as when I hug Carrick, but at least he's trying.

For the longest time, my dad didn't visit me. When I was a kid, I thought if I was good enough at fighting and all the stuff my mentors Si and Jeff were teaching me, maybe he'd visit.

Needless to say, it didn't work. I did end up being a kick-ass fighter though, so I guess I have my dad to thank for that. It's only been since I turned out to be the not-so-last dragon that he's started paying attention to me. He needed me for his failed revolution, and I helped him turn into a proper Chameleon for the first time.

I guess you could say our relationship is a work in progress.

"I can see by your expression you're on the verge of giving up, but I'm here to tell you, don't."

Stepping back, I raise my eyebrows at him. "Why not? It seems pretty straightforward."

"The Mountain supers, they can be pedantic. And while they mostly get their information right, they also don't know everything. There is still a chance we can change this around. This isn't the end."

I nod carefully, acknowledging to myself that he's saying exactly what I want to hear. But is he saying it to keep my hopes up, and thereby make my last days bearable? Or because he really believes that there's a way out of this?

I don't know.

"What do you suggest we do? Carrick can't read the Earthbound texts. They won't be able to figure them out for weeks, they said. I got the impression from his grandfather...." I can't quite bring myself to say the words.

"That your demise is imminent?" Dad shakes his head. "That old man has been a drama queen for as long as I've known him. We'll find a way out of this. You wait and see."

Tears well in my eyes, and I lean into his arms again. He wraps me up tightly, and I cling to him, desperate to believe that he's right, and this isn't the end of the road for me.

"What's the first thing we do?" I say, between sniffing.

"We find some records we can search. Something that was around at the time the original spell web was put in place."

"And that would be...?" I think of all the records down below this place. None of them are useable.

"Zane's clan has a secret hold not far from here. He came with me and has agreed to take you to see it. He thinks there might be some records we could look at that could be useful."

"Zane? Where is he?" I glance over my dad's shoulder,

half expecting to see the older dragon at the entrance to the garden. I kind of miss him.

"I asked him to give us some time alone together. I wasn't sure how you'd be."

"And how am I?" I ask drily.

"As well as can be expected." A buzzing sound in Dad's pocket distracts us both, and he pulls out a small black phone. He looks down at the number with a puzzled expression.

"Someone you don't like?" I ask.

"The last person I would have expected," he says slowly.

"Are you going to answer it?"

He blinks at me, and then down at the phone. Then he presses the button and puts the phone to his ear. "Afternoon, Director."

I sit back down on the bench abruptly. *The director?*

Who the hell does he think he is, calling Dad like this? He tried to kill us all. He handed Dad over to the Earthbound, let Vincent do whatever he wanted with him.

"Tell him to shove off," I whisper loudly to my father.

"That's a very interesting proposal," says Damien slowly. His expression is surprised.

"Tell him if I see him again I'm going to toast him like a marshmallow," I say.

Damien just shushes me by waving his hand in my direction. "Certainly, Director. We'd be happy to meet with you."

Meet with him? "Tell him the only place we'll meet him is *in hell*," I say, incensed.

"Headquarters? As long as you can guarantee our safety, we'd be prepared to meet with you. When suits?" He listens again. "Tomorrow is perfect. We'll see you there." He hangs up the phone.

"*We'll see him*? Tomorrow?"

"He wants to talk. He has a proposal for us to consider. It can't hurt to talk to the man. You never know, he might have some information that's useful to us."

"But he's our enemy. He gave you to Vincent. He was *in league* with Vincent."

"He's a powerful man, Mei. Never underestimate him."

"What does he want from you?"

Damien shakes his head. "Not me. *You.* He wants you to work for him. He wants the power of the spell web in his hands."

"Ha. He's gonna cry when we tell him what's happening," I say.

My father shakes his head. "We're not going to breathe a word of your situation to anyone." He looks sternly down at me. "I mean it, Mei. That kind of information could cause mass hysteria."

"I thought you were all for living without the spell web?"

Dad lets out a big gust of breath. "I thought it would be the answer to everything. Now I'm not so sure." Shadows appear in his eyes, and I know he's remembering all the people who died for his cause.

"Really?" It's the complete opposite to everything my father was trying to put in place. Everything we fought for, everything that Roger and the others died for.

"I've experienced life without the spell web, and it was never an easy place to live. I much prefer the calm of having you in charge of it. You don't use too much of it like the Earthbound did."

"What happens when I die? If not now, then later, when I'm old?"

He shrugs. "That's a problem we're going to have to work on together. We'll find a way."

"Are you really that sure about it?" I ask, hesitating. "There don't seem to be too many options right now."

"I am. There are many things between heaven and earth. Something out there will help us."

"Like the director?"

"Maybe the director. Maybe something else. We're not going to sit back and just believe some old dude who thinks he knows everything."

Warmth fills my chest. I didn't have him around growing up, but I'm kinda getting used to having him around now. He's the only one so far who's given me hope that maybe I might make it out of this alive. "Okay. Sounds good."

13

I'm in the air again, this time with Zane flying at my side. Carrick is on his back; my father is on my back. We're almost in New York, a much faster journey than my first visit to the SIG Headquarters with Seth.

I allow myself a tiny pang at the absence of Seth. I didn't even get to tell him where we're going. He's still dealing with his Raven clan issues, and my father wouldn't let me tell him what we were doing over the phone. Part of me wants to obsess over it, to wonder what's happening that Seth is clearly not telling me. But right now, I can't let it distract me, so I focus my thoughts on our mission ahead. The director is expecting us. He wants the power of the spell web.

And he's a tricky bastard.

Damien has already given me a big speech about being careful and not taking any risks. Apparently he's worried. It's nice. Even if it's completely pointless.

I fly down, below the clouds, to check our position. We're almost there. We've decided to land nearby, in Central Park, before changing and heading to the SIG building. The spell web is whirling around inside me, working overtime, protecting us from being visible to the humans. The magic is heavy inside me, like a weight I can't throw off. I feel the magic of all the supernaturals living in New York, their energy attracted to the spell web like metal to a magnet. I can pull on their magic at any time, use it for myself.

Except I won't.

Even if using it didn't mean I'd have another attack, I wouldn't do it. I wouldn't abuse the spell web like the Earth-bound did. I refuse to be like Vincent.

So we sail in, almost silent, the magic swirling around us in the early morning sky. I land without a sound, Zane beside me, his expression grim. He's here against his will. He voted to blow up the SIG headquarters rather than talk with the director.

I'm leaning in the same direction. But my father convinced us both that we need to talk to him first. We can blow him up later.

There's a chill in the air, and I change quickly into my floaty cotton pants and black T-shirt, wishing I'd thought to bring a sweatshirt. It didn't seem that cold in the desert. I rub my arms to get rid of the goose bumps.

"You'll warm up soon enough," says my father, glancing over at me. He's got a thick down jacket on to keep him warm for the flight, so I make a face to show what I think of his comment. He shrugs and strides off down a path toward Central Park West, leading and assuming we'll follow. Carrick strides off after him, like it's the most natural thing in the world. I glance over at Zane, who's frowning back at me. I shrug. My father's never going to change. He just takes the lead and expects others to follow him.

Mostly it works out.

I think of our recent rebellion efforts. Sometimes it doesn't.

I guess Zane is thinking the same thing. We ended up burying a lot of people who didn't deserve to die because of the leadership of my father and the others. Should we really be trusting him again so soon? I hesitate for a moment longer.

But we need information. And this is simply a fact-gathering mission, not an attack, or a political foray. I sigh and move off after my father, feeling Zane move into place behind me. His agitation makes the air crackle around us, but I don't say anything. I understand his frustration, but I don't have a solution for it. I'm just glad he's here, helping out.

We catch up to the others and cross at the lights together. My father walks with a jaunty step, Carrick with long, purposeful strides. I've learned not to trust the external appearance of either of them. They're both masters at hiding their true emotions under a facade.

Zane and I, the dragons of the group, are less proficient. Zane's dragon magic is building up inside him, and I flick him a quick warning glance. His eyes are flashing with fire.

"Stay calm, Zane. We need to get through this without incident," I say in a low voice.

"What is there to be calm about? We're heading into the enemy's territory, knowing there will be a who-knows-what kind of trap, with only a hope and a prayer."

"Dad knows these people. He knows what they're like. And he's a master at getting what he wants."

"Like he did with the revolution?"

"That was bigger, too big maybe. On this level, one-to-one, you can't beat him." *I hope.*

Zane gives me a look, but his eyes become less wild, and the muscles in his shoulders relax slightly. He's willing to believe me for now.

This is the first time I've seen the outside the SIG building properly. It's a brownstone building, twelve stories high, with ornate, carved stone. It looks like just another high-end apartment building on the edge of Central Park with a small red canopy over the entrance and a guard standing at the door.

But when my father goes up to the guard, the man looks a little too alert to be the sleepy doorman of an apartment building. He asks for ID and takes a thumbprint on a tiny device he pulls out of his pocket.

The device glows green. The guard opens the door, and we all walk in after my father.

We're in a large foyer with marble everywhere. At the far end, looking sternly at us over a reception counter is an older man wearing a blue suit so perfectly it's obvious he's some kind of ex-military officer.

"Damien," he says sternly. "You're back." He glances around at the rest of us. "And you brought friends."

"The director is expecting us," says Damien casually.

"He certainly is," mutters the old man. He glares at my father. "I hope you know what you're letting yourself in for, son."

"That bad, huh?" says Dad.

"Worse." He glares at the rest of us like we're naughty kids and he's the school principal, and then he waves us toward the elevators. "Head down to level five. He's expecting you."

Level five? Down? I glance at my father. How much space does one secret government organization need? Apparently more than I thought.

We crowd into the elevator, and Carrick presses five. It doesn't light up and the car stays where it is.

"I think I have to do it," says Dad. He leans over and

places his finger squarely on the button. It lights up an ominous red, and the elevator car starts moving down.

"Am I the only one creeped out by that?" I ask.

"I'm the only one on file. It's fine, just a security precaution."

I give my father a look that says just what I think of their security precautions. How easy is it going to be for them to trap us down here? No wonder Jeff never let me come here when I was a kid. He would have deemed it utterly unsafe.

I lift myself onto the balls of my feet, bouncing lightly from side to side, preparing for a fight. I'm trying to be subtle about it, but when Carrick glances my way and looks pointedly down at my feet, I realize it's pretty obvious. But I don't stop.

The car comes to a halt, and the doors open.

14

The director is standing outside the elevator, waiting for us. He looks just the same, dressed in a suit, his little piggy eyes looking over all of us as if assessing our value.

There's a flash of something in his expression when his gaze passes over me, but it's gone so fast, I might've imagined it. I examine him closely, trying to find the goodness in him, trying to find the part of him that was able to raise a daughter like Liling. She was so smart, so kind and gentle. It doesn't seem to match up at all.

"Welcome to you all, thank you for visiting me," he says, holding his hands out wide as if he's a king and this is his domain. I guess it's true.

He steps forward and shakes Dad's hand like they're life-long pals. Dad shakes back, a little more reserved.

"I wasn't sure you'd convince your... friends... to come with you, Damien." He glances around again, skimming over Zane and me like he doesn't want to look too closely. Carrick shifts restlessly next to me. The director doesn't offer to shake anyone else's hands. Given Carrick's status as the Mountain king, it's a serious breach of protocol.

The hairs on the back of my neck rise up, and I'm immediately even more on edge. This guy is definitely planning something.

Then make sure he doesn't get away with it, says a familiar voice in my head. Jeff. He's long dead, but the lessons he gave me from the time I was twelve have stood the test of time. I do a scan of the area, noting the long hallway in one direction, how many doors (five), the light fixtures (nothing special), and alternate exits (maybe through the ceiling cavity).

"Come, let's discuss my proposal." The director gestures to a door just down from the elevators. Dad leads the way, and we all follow, some of us more reluctantly than others. I fall to the back of the group, watching closely.

The room is large enough for a boardroom table that seats twenty, and a minibar along the side.

"Would anyone like a drink?" asks the director, gesturing to an attractive dark-haired woman standing beside the table. "Anna will get you whatever you'd like."

"Coffee would be perfect," says Damien, and we all mutter our agreement. The woman nods and smiles, then walks to the bar, which turns out to have a fancy coffee machine hidden behind it.

"Come, let's sit. Was it a long flight?" The director takes the seat at the head of the table, leaving us to scatter around the table in front of him.

Damien smiles. "It took a while," he says in a noncommittal voice as he sits. "Although everything is much closer when you fly dragon-back."

The coffee machine starts whirring in the background,

and the director smiles tightly at Damien. "So pleased for you."

"How are things at the SIG these days? Now that the spell web is back in place?" asks Damien.

"It's what we always wanted. For things to be back to normal, so we can all get on with our lives," says the director smoothly. "You seem to have returned easily enough to the other side of your rebellion?" He cocks an eyebrow at my father.

"And you seemed to enjoy putting people in prison when the spell web was down." I can't help it; the words just pop out of my mouth.

The director's face darkens, and he looks at me properly for the first time. "We were forced into those actions by you, young lady. You were the one who broke the power structure, who tore down the spell web in the first place."

"Only because Vincent—"

Dad holds up his hands in a shushing motion. "Let's not get embroiled in the politics of what has passed us by already. What's done is done. We're here to discuss the future."

Every instinct inside me is roaring that I should change into a dragon right now and cover this place in flames. It's not exactly subtle. But one look at my father's face is enough to hold me back, to keep my instincts under control. He wants to keep this discussion polite, and I need to do my best to help him.

Anna comes around the table and hands out our cups of delicious-smelling coffee. They're all barista style, with a flower pattern on the top, and a divine scent that drifts past my nose. I let my coffee sit on the table for a moment, letting the rich aroma roll over me, but Carrick and Zane take sips from theirs straight away.

I notice my father leaves his cup on the table.

"So, tell us about your proposal, Director," says my father, leaning back in his chair. He's so at ease; he looks like he's on holiday. Except these days I can tell it's all an act. He's seriously worried. Something is wrong about this whole situation. Before we arrived my father assumed he could handle whatever was thrown at us.

But now, something has changed.

I watch the director closely, trying to figure out what my father has sensed, but nothing is immediately obvious. That he doesn't like me is clear. Is he upset that Liling joined our side of the battle while the spell web was down? Does he even care that she died? I don't know the answer.

The director leans forward, putting his forearms down on the table. "We'd like you to come back into the fold, Damien. You and Mei. We'd like both of you to work for the SIG, help us keep everything calm."

I blink and give my head a small shake. Did I hear that wrong? "You want me to work for you? After everything that's happened?"

"I'm willing to put our past... disagreements... behind us and work together. We all want the same thing."

"Do you really think that's a good idea?" says Damien carefully. "Mei is still considered enemy number one in many places." He's being very diplomatic. And ignoring the fact that I'd never work for this slimeball in a million years.

"We'd be able to handle it. She's the spell web, our most treasured asset. We wouldn't let anyone hurt her."

It sounds like he wants to lock me up and throw away the key. I glance at my father, and he gives a tiny shake of his head. He wants me to keep quiet.

Which would be fine, if my dragon senses weren't still roaring and pounding and growling at me. If my whole body didn't feel like it wanted to burst out of this human shell and take my true form, just so I could burn the director to a crisp. And maybe that Anna girl, who's smirking at me from beside the coffee machine.

Wait.

She's smirking.

I look down at my untouched coffee and take a sniff. Too late, I realize that under the soothing tones of roasted coffee, there's something else.

Something off.

They're trying to drug us.

15

Zane has his cup raised, about to take another sip, and Carrick has half finished his coffee. His eyes are drooping just a little, and my heart drops. I take another sniff, and a subvocal growl makes its way up my throat.

I look at my father, and realize this is what he saw, what made him so concerned. He clearly wasn't expecting such a blatant attack. His face is still bland, and he catches me watching him. He gives me a look that I don't understand and turns his attention back to the director. I think he's telling me to keep quiet, but I can't let the others just keep drinking the drugged coffee.

I clear my throat. "Zane?" I say, trying for a casual tone. "Would you like to join the SIG too?"

Zane puts down his cup, his movements awkward and a little groggy. He's already had enough to create a problem. "No way," he says, a slight slur in his voice. He blinks and looks surprised.

"I'm sorry, that's not the offer on the table. I can't have a whole bunch of rogue—" The director clears his throat. "—*unauthorized* dragons roaming about, causing trouble."

I glare at the director. He couldn't make his dislike of dragons any clearer. His offer is clearly bogus, so why is Dad going along with it like this? Why isn't he standing up and meeting the director head on?

"Why do you want *me,* then?" I ask as sweetly as I can. I'm pretty much the definition of rogue.

The director looks at my untouched cup of coffee and frowns. "You're different from the rest."

"Because you think you'll be able to influence me, and therefore the spell web?" I ask still trying for sweetness. "I'm not that easily controlled."

Across the table, Carrick slowly slumps down until his head is resting awkwardly on the table. Zane looks groggily over at him, and then back at me. He blinks slowly.

I stand up, pushing my chair out behind me. I've had enough.

"I'm sure we could come to some kind of—"

"We might have been able to, perhaps, if you hadn't just tried to *drug* us," I say, my voice a growl. "But now that you've made the first move against us, you can stuff any kind of cooperation between us where the sun don't shine."

"Mei—" My father tries to hold up my tirade.

"He tried to *drug* us," I repeat, gesturing toward Carrick and Zane, who are now both lying head down on the table, snoring gently. My every instinct is to transform and fight back. I can feel the heat licking my body, and I'm sure my eyes are filled with dragon fire. My hands clench at my sides as I fight with myself.

"Did you drink it?" asks the director smoothly.

"Of course not."

"And neither did your father. It's those kinds of smarts

that we need in SIG agents. You don't think like other people. You don't assume. *That's* why we want you on our team."

It's very smoothly done, and I hesitate, wondering if he's really that manipulative. But the look of shock on Anna's face is enough to convince me that he's just a smooth liar. "Are they going to be okay?"

"They'll have a headache when they wake in about an hour," says the director. "In the meantime, I can show you around. We've made some changes since you were here last."

"I'm not going anywhere, except out of here. You can't just *drug* people." I'm getting a little hysterical, but he's acting like it's just an ordinary occurrence.

"It was a test, a way to be sure that we were making the right offer," says the director. "It's very common. Isn't that right, Damien?"

My father's face is so mild, it sends a chill over me. That's when he's at his worst. "The director has been known to use this kind of test in the past," he agrees.

"If they're not okay in an hour...." Even as I say the words, my dragon side is resisting the capitulation. My whole body is straining against my control, wanting to change. Damien shifts in his chair, and I know it's a warning to me to keep my dragon contained. Fire is burning inside me, washing over my body like a sea of flames, and everything just wants to give in to the urge.

The director just looks at me calmly. "I promise, they will have no lasting effects. My people will take care of them while I show you around."

"Mei, they'll be fine," says my father in a soothing voice.

I glare at him, but manage to take a deep breath, and then another. The fire dies down a little, allowing me to think it through. "Just so you know, it's not normal behaviour to drug people and act as if it's some kind of test," I say, refusing to play their mind games.

"We're not a normal kind of organization. And these are not normal times," replies the director. "What do you say to my offer so far?"

"We'd like access to the SIG archives," I say, instead of what I'm really thinking.

"Once you've signed on as SIG agents, you will of course be granted access."

My father stands up, his expression easy and uncomplicated. That in itself calms me down. Damien's so pissed off that he's actually smiling like a friendly old grandfather at the director. He's planning something so diabolical it will make the director regret the day he pulled a trick like this. "Show us some of these changes," he says. "I'm curious."

The director gestures for us to precede him through the doors and into the hallway. I follow the line of doors down to the end and turn, finding another corridor. This one has no doors, except at either end.

"We're doing some complicated research," the director is saying. "Based on the work of one of your recruits, Damien."

"Oh, really?" says my father blandly. He looks like butter wouldn't melt in his mouth, but white chameleon scales are forming on the back of his hand. They disappear again quickly, but it tells me how close to the edge he is. At least I'm not the only one who finds this situation intolerable.

"Yes, Hazel is proving to be a valuable asset. Her work with demons is incomparable."

My heart leaps. Demons. This is exactly the kind of thing we need information on. "Can we meet her?" I ask, trying to sound casual.

"Your father has already met Hazel, but I'm sure she'd

love to meet you, Mei. I'll take you to her research lab." The director barely manages to hide a smirk as he looks over at my father.

Dad smiles at the director with such a mild expression it raises all the hairs on the back of my neck.

The director is so fucked.

16

"Hazel, this is Mei. And you already know Mei's father, Damien Walker," says the director, gesturing toward a short, attractive woman with glasses, wearing ripped jeans and a Firefly T-shirt. She's standing in the middle of a pristine research lab, and looks more like a graduate research assistant who lives on ramen noodles and frozen peas than someone who's in charge. She doesn't look at all like the typical SIG agents I've met either. In fact she doesn't look old enough to be an SIG agent. The spell web flickers around her, dancing over magic that's visible to my eyes only.

Hazel smiles warmly at my father. "It's good to see you, Damien. I thought I'd never see you again, after...." She trails off, and her smile falters.

Damien moves closer and holds out one hand. "It's good to see you safe and sound, Hazel. I was worried."

"We managed to survive," she murmurs with a quick glance at the director as she shakes my father's hand. "What the hell," she says, and then leans in to give Damien a hug. There's some kind of silent communication between them that I don't understand. Hopefully it's to make sure Hazel will help us.

"Hi," I say when she moves back out of the hug. I hold out my hand and take hers in a firm grip. "Nice to meet you."

"Likewise." She's staring at me curiously, like I'm a bug under a microscope.

"I hear my father recruited you?"

Hazel grins. "He did."

"And you're working with demons?"

"She *controls* them," says Damien. "Hazel is a chalice."

For the second time today, my heart skips a beat. This is the second time I've heard the word in as many days. Except Seth's dad told us the last chalice died years ago. "That's rare, right?" I ask Hazel.

"I don't really know," she glances at Damien for confirmation, and he nods. "They tell me I'm unique."

I look at her closely, trying to see what it is about her that's so unique. "What exactly is it that you do with demons?"

Hazel shrugs. "Demons are attracted to me. Like Damien said, I can control them... and destroy them when everything else is going okay around me."

"She's also a talented inventor," adds the director. "She's developed several devices that help with demons."

"Wow, that's amazing," I say, thinking of the last time I spent time with a demon. It was big and scary and tried to kill me. It almost succeeded.

"We're working on ways to amp up my abilities, to allow me to control more demons at one time," Hazel is saying. She glances at the director. "Maybe even use their energy for different purposes, if we can get it stable enough."

"Because of the demon plague?" I say, pretending it's old news and not gossip I'm trying to confirm.

"Yes. Precisely," says Hazel with a smile, like I'm a kid who's done well in class.

And with those two words, she confirms my worst nightmares. Evan was right, there is a demon problem. Could he also be right that it will be worse than anything we've seen so far?

At least he was wrong about there being no more chalices.

The director clears his throat. "Well, Hazel, we must be off. We'll let you get back to your work."

She waves one hand absently and turns back to her microscope as we leave the room.

"Do you have many people working on demons?" I ask as the director closes the door behind us. Maybe I don't have to worry about the demon plague. Maybe the SIG has it under control.

"No. Hazel, as she said, is unique. Special." The director turns to look at me. "As are you, Mei."

"Is that why you want me to work for you? Because I'm unique?"

"It's our responsibility to ensure the safety of everyone around us, both humans and supernaturals. It's what we've been doing all these years—until the spell web was destroyed."

"By me."

"By you."

"So why is having me in the SIG so important for you?"

"Do I really have to answer that question? You're smart." The director gets a calculating look in his eyes. "As is Seth. We'd be prepared to offer him his old job back here as well, despite his previous... insubordination."

My ears prick up at this news. Seth was gutted when he lost his place at the SIG. He did what he considered the right thing at the time, but he lost his identity as an agent, and it was hard on him. Would he want his job back again? To be reinstated back into his previous life?

I think of the one-eyed pirate he's become and struggle to imagine him wearing the tidy suit and tie that the director and the other agents we've seen have all been wearing. Only Hazel—in her more casual clothes—is an indication of a possible change in tone around here.

"I'd have to talk to him, see if that's something he'd want."

"It would be conditional on you joining us as well, Mei," the director says with a warning in his voice.

I nod. Message received. Seth being reinstated is supposed to be another sweetener in the pot for me. I bite my lip absently, staring around the hallway, trying to figure out what's wrong with everything here. Why does it all feel strange? The spell web is buzzing inside me, but I ignore it. Using it will only bring on another attack.

"Do you have any other conditions we should know about?" asks my father as we pass through some fire doors and go deeper into the building.

The director waves me forward down a brightly lit hallway. "My only other requirement is rather boring, I'm afraid. It's about asset management. I would require you to hand over the running of the Earthbound compound to my people."

Again, I'm about to yell, 'Hell no!' when I see my father shaking his head at me. He's telling me to calm down and lead the director on for a bit longer. I never would have expected this to be so difficult. I clear my throat, attempting to push down my objections. "Really? I feel like it's in good hands at the moment," I say instead. "Why do you feel you should be in charge of it?"

"We have the personnel, the know-how. It's an important building, filled with knowledge we don't wish to lose."

I take a breath, as if I'm considering it. In reality, I'm just trying to make sure I say the right thing. This feels like a dangerous dance, where I'm being expected to lead, but don't know the steps, or even recognize the music. All I know is that it feels like it's life or death. My father is brewing something... and so is the director. "Perhaps you could work alongside the Mountain supers?" I ask, glancing at my father as I talk. He isn't giving me anything to work with.

The director's face darkens as he takes in my words, and he shakes his head. "I'm afraid it's a nonnegotiable requirement. We require the Earthbound compound."

He's leading us along another hallway toward a set of thick steel doors. Something important is behind these doors. I try to keep my mind on the conversation, and not get distracted wondering what's behind them.

"Why do you need it?"

His eye twitches, as if he's annoyed I even get to ask the question. He pulls a small object out of his pocket and presses a button. The heavy steel doors in front of us open slowly, and again I lead the way into the new room.

It's small space, with a table and chairs in the middle, and beds to one side. Zane and Carrick are laid out on a bed each.

"Are they okay—?" It's only as I turn that I realize the director has retreated from the room, and the steel doors are returning to their original locked position.

"I'm sorry, Damien, Mei. Given your responses today, this is the only way," says the director through the closing doors. His voice is thick with smug satisfaction.

My father stands near Zane and Carrick, staring down at

their unconscious faces. "He's locked us in," he says absently, as if that's not the worst of our problems.

"How are we going to get out?"

"We're not. We're locked securely in here. He's done an excellent job of making it dragon escape proof."

17

I walk around the perimeter of the room again, examining every inch of it. "He never expected us to agree to his deal, did he?"

"No. It was always a trap."

"You knew it was a trap, though?"

"Of course. Didn't you?"

"I *thought* it was, but I figured you had some kind of sneaky plan."

"I always have a sneaky plan," he says with a tiny smile that fades away to nothing. "The director is not forgiving. He blames you for Liling's death. He would no more work with you than he would a demon."

"Then why did you convince me to come here?" I say, exasperated.

"Because I needed to see what he was doing. Whether he really did expect to control demons."

"Through Hazel?"

"Yes."

"And what have you decided?"

"That he's dangerous. He's going to lead us into a terrifying demon apocalypse if we don't stop him."

"With help from your friend Hazel?"

He shakes his head. "She won't help him, not once she realizes what he's up to."

I sit down on a chair, letting out a huff of breath as I do so. "Then what are we going to do now? How do we get out of here?"

"The same way you got out of the SIG headquarters last time."

I frown, thinking back. "With gas masks and knockout gas?"

"With a little help from our friends," says Damien softly.

"Could you be any more cryptic?" I say in exasperation.

My father looks up into the corners of the room, to the small cameras that are scattered around the room. "There's a reason for that."

I roll my eyes at him. "So we wait?"

"We wait."

"Can we talk about demons?"

"What about them?"

"Is one chalice enough to control a demon plague?"

He hesitates, and that's an answer by itself. "I honestly don't know. Hazel hasn't been raised to be a chalice. Their kind was thought to have been wiped out years ago. There are others who are helping her learn, but...."

"How come there are so many demons all of a sudden?"

"It's not sudden. It's just been surreptitious. Only in certain areas, and helped by one particular man."

"Who?"

He shakes his head. "No one you know. An old enemy of Hazel's who will do almost anything to get his hands on her powers. He's the one who put the idea of using demons as an energy source into the director's head."

"And that's what you think the director wants to use Hazel for?"

"She confirmed it herself. I think she already knows there's a problem. She's a smart kid, that's why she mentioned it to you."

There's a moan from the bed beside us, and Carrick opens his eyes. "Wha' happen'?" he says.

I stand up and go over to him. "It's okay, you should be fine. The director tried to drug us."

"You din' drink?" says Carrick, putting one hand to his head like it's painful.

"Nope. Too suspicious."

Another groan announces Zane is waking up too.

"Good, now they're both awake, we can begin our rescue attempt," says Damien.

"I thought we had to wait on someone else letting us out?" I say.

"We do. But we can make it easier for them. Help me over here would you?" He starts pulling the chairs away from the table. I shrug at Carrick, who's still lying on his bed.

"What are we doing this for, exactly?"

"Distraction," says Damien in a low voice next to my ear. "I just want whoever is watching us via the video feed to think we're planning something. Freak them out a little."

"So they'll focus on us, and not on wherever else our helpers are?" I whisper back.

"Precisely."

I take one end of the table and help him move it to a spot underneath one of the cameras. "Should I destroy it?" I ask.

He shrugs. "If you want."

I climb up onto the table and peer at the tiny camera. It's held in a glass bubble with a metal covering at the back. I tug on it experimentally. It looks like an upgraded version of the one they were using last time I was here. That time I just hung off it, and it came away from the wall.

A red light starts flashing on the side of the camera, and then a buzz of electricity appears over the metal and glass bubble casing.

They've electrified it. I step back, tempted to use some of the spell web magic to make it burn. But that's not the point of what I'm doing. It's a distraction. I need something that will keep them occupied watching me for longer. I jump down off the table again and grab one of the chairs. Hefting it up onto the table, I lift it up high and bring it down on the camera. The glass shatters, and the metal bends.

The benefits of being a dragon.

"Oops," I say, grinning down at the camera. The buzz of electricity is gone.

"What are you doing up there?" asks Carrick, who is now standing unsteadily next to his bed. "Do you need help?"

"No, you just get yourself feeling better again. Maybe they could bring us some food?" I ask, turning back to the camera, as if I'm asking it the question.

My father is over in a different corner, fiddling around with the air vents. They're too small for us to crawl through, so I don't know quite what he's planning. But I'm determined to keep their attention on me instead of him.

Simple is always best, as Jeff used to say.

I pull on the camera, and it whines a little in its socket. What if this sends them to us? I glance over at my father. Is that part of the plan? I'm not entirely certain about what my part in this plan is supposed to be. That's the trouble with working alongside Damien. He's got more freaking layers than an onion, and more balls in the air than a circus clown.

Then I shrug. I figure he knows me well enough to gauge what I might do in this situation. I pull on the camera again, and it comes out of the wall. I yank on the wires coming through the wall, pulling them away from the rest of the set up. The light on the camera is dead, and they can't see me anymore.

Is that going to make them head over here? I turn around. Not really, given that the other four cameras in the room are now trained on me. They haven't lost their ability to see me. Not yet.

I jump down off the table, happy to just be doing something. Especially something a little destructive if I'm honest. This place gives me the creeps.

I drag the table over to the next camera, making my movements slower and more theatrical than they strictly need to be. Giving them a show, while the real action takes place over by my father.

The table crashes noisily into the metal wall underneath the next camera, and I allow myself a little grin. My dragon self appreciates the chaos. If Seth were here, he'd appreciate it too. My chest tightens, and my grin falls. I hope he's okay —although wherever he is, I'm sure it can't be as bad as being locked up at the SIG headquarters.

I'm not entirely sure how I managed to get into this position for a second time in my life.

I've just climbed back up on the table when there's a loud click at the main doors. The mechanism has been unlocked. They're opening slowly inwards, and I crane my neck to see who's come visiting this time. Am I about to be taken down a notch for the destruction of the cameras?

There's no one there. No one comes into our little prison.

"Come on, Mei. This is it. We have to move." My father gestures at me, as he runs toward the exit, Carrick and Zane just behind him. They're almost there when the doors start to close again. I leap off the table, sprinting after them. Dad gets through, Carrick just behind him. Zane turns and tries to hold the doors open for me. They're too big and keep closing inexorably shut.

I'm sprinting as hard as I can, my legs pounding over the metal floor. It's going to be close. At last second, I manage to slip in past Zane, and drag him through with me. Before I can do more than take a breath, Dad is pulling me by my arm, dragging me down the corridor.

"We don't have long. This isn't as well organized as the last rescue."

"We barely made it out that time," I huff at him.

"Then all the more reason to concentrate harder," he replies.

18

We sprint down the corridor, through a set of fire doors, and into another hallway. At the end, there's a foyer, and we hesitate.

"Which way?" I ask Damien.

He looks at the three options in front of us. One hallway and two doors.

"Over here," calls a small voice behind us.

I turn, and there's Hazel, poking her head through what looks like a secret door that's been built directly into the wall.

"What the hell?"

Dad moves over to her. "What are you doing?" he whispers. "You shouldn't be putting yourself in danger like this."

"How else am I supposed to get you out of here?"

"You were supposed to call someone else."

Hazel gives him a look and shakes her head. "It's like you don't know me at all," she says. "I thought we were friends."

I give a muffled snort of laughter. "I like her, Dad. She's a keeper."

He glares back at me, but there's laughter in his eyes as well. "She reminds me of you," he says.

"She must be amazing," I retort.

"Come on, we don't have time for this," says Hazel, gesturing at us to come through the panel in the wall. "I called the person you asked me to. He'll be here soon. But I needed to act before he arrived. They were planning.... Anyway, it doesn't matter. But it won't take long for them to discover that someone has messed with their systems. You need to be gone before that happens." We all crawl inside the gap in the wall, Carrick struggling to get his huge body through. Soon we're all standing in a dusty cavity in the wall, watching as Hazel returns the panel to its place.

"Come on, follow me," says Hazel, as she dusts off her hands.

She leads the way, walking quickly into the darkness of the hollow section of wall. It gets narrower the further along we go.

"How did you know about that secret door?" I ask in a whisper.

Hazel shrugged. "I made it. Just in case. You never know when you're going to have to get out of a place like this quickly."

I look with wide eyes at my father. "Is she always like this?"

He just grins.

A minute later Hazel stops alongside another wall panel. "I'm going to go through first, just in case. The director is already suspicious of me. He might think to check my lab first."

She pries open the panel with a tiny Swiss army knife and pokes her head through. We all wait impatiently in the darkness. A sneeze builds up in my nose from the dust. I hold it in until Hazel comes back.

"It's safe. Come on out."

I sneeze in answer.

Zane gives me a look and steps out first, followed by my father and then Carrick. I go last and help Hazel to put the panel back in place.

"How are we going to get out of here?" I ask, recognizing Hazel's lab from earlier. It's not like we can go up in the elevators. Unless she can do something with them as well?

"There's a supply lift for the lab. It'll get you to the main level. From there you just have to get outside." She glances at me. "You can fly, right?"

I nod. "Zane and I are both dragons."

"Good," she says, looking at me curiously like she's looking for wings or scales. "Then you'll be fine. I've got another distraction planned to keep them hunting in the wrong direction." She's all business as she leads the way through the tables set up with scientific equipment.

"Are you going to be okay staying here?" I ask. "Maybe you should come with us?"

Hazel shakes her head. "No, I have to stay here. I've got some things I want to do before I vanish." She says it so confidently, I know she's done it before, and she's got it all planned to do it again. She leads us to a tiny half-sized elevator sitting in the far corner. "Hopefully you'll all fit," she says, looking carefully at Carrick. The door reaches Carrick's waist.

"We can go in two loads," says Damien. "One dragon, one passenger. Carrick, you go with Mei. Once you get to the top, leave straight away," he says.

Carrick shakes his head. "No, I'll go second. You and Mei are more important in all of this than us."

"Not me," says my father, a spark of anger in his voice for the first time. "*You're* the Mountain king. I shouldn't have brought you with me on this mission. I only realized how stupid that was when I saw you passed out on the table back there. I'm sorry."

Carrick shook his head. "It's my job to protect Mei and the spell web. I would have insisted on coming."

"Then protect her now for me. Go first. Leave as soon as you get up there. We'll be right behind you."

"What I liked best about that whole conversation is that I wasn't included in it," I say musingly to Hazel.

"I did notice, but didn't want to mention it," she replies with a grin. "Although, to be fair, you *are* the spell web. Having battled through the times without the spell web, I'm eager to keep it in place."

"As good a reason as any to survive," I say grimly. Without looking back at anyone, I climb into the tiny lift space and crawl as far to the side as I can. Carrick crawls in with me, scrunched up into as much of a ball as he can make himself.

Hazel pokes her head through the door opening. "I'll press the button for Ground. Get out as fast as you can. I don't think there will be anyone up there in the storage area, but I can't guarantee it. Be prepared for anything." She shuts the door firmly before we can say anything else. I don't even get to say goodbye to my dad. Silence hangs heavy around us for a moment as the old elevator carriage moves upward.

"We gotta stop meeting like this," I say to Carrick.

"Someday, we're going to be able to have a normal life," he mutters. "With less mortal peril."

I feel a pang, knowing that my chances of having a normal life became nonexistent as soon as I became the spell web. "It'd be too boring," I say lightly. I might not have this crazy life for much longer either.

But I can't think about that right now. "Game face," I say. "We're almost there. Be ready for anything."

The carriage bumps to a stop, and the light for the Ground floor goes off. The doors open, and Carrick crawls out. I'm following him on my hands and knees when he stiffens.

"What are you doing here?" he says to someone standing just past my line of sight.

19

I scramble to my feet, panic flaring, my magic bursting to get out. I search past Carrick's bulk for whoever is confronting us.

A familiar thatch of brown hair comes into view. My breath escapes in a whoosh, and I push past Carrick to slam into Seth's arms. His warm smoky scent curls into my senses, and I take a deep breath. It feels like home.

Carrick claps Seth on the arm. "It's good to see you," he says.

"I wish it could be in better circumstances," says Seth.

"What *are* you doing here?" I ask against his chest.

"Some woman called Hazel called me," he says shortly. "More important, what are *you* doing here?" I look up and see the flames in his eyes. He's pissed at me, even though he's holding me tight against him like he doesn't want to let me go.

"The director phoned Dad and said he had an offer. It seemed like an opportunity to find out some information."

"You didn't think to call me?" His voice vibrates with... hurt?

I hesitate. "I did call you. You didn't answer."

"You should have let your father come alone. You didn't need to put yourself in danger like this."

I frown. Since Jeff died, everyone is always trying to save me from harm. It gets old after a while. "I'm not a child, Seth. You can't protect me from everything."

"Still—"

Carrick steps forward. "You two need to argue about this later on. Right now, we gotta get out of here."

Seth's arms tighten around me, and then he lets me go. "Carrick's right. We don't have time to wait around."

"We have to wait for Dad and Zane," I say, glancing back at the tiny freight elevator.

Carrick shakes his head. "That's exactly why your father gave me the instructions, not you. We can't wait for them."

"But—"

"We need to get out of here. We'll be safer in two smaller groups."

Seth puts his hands on my shoulders and forces me to look up at him. "Mei. Think it through. Your father is the best strategist we know. If he told you to go, we go." His words break through the mass of objections in my head.

"I guess." I hate the idea of leaving Dad and Zane. But Carrick has a point about being safer in smaller groups. It might actually be easier for them to escape without me.

"How do we get out of here?" Carrick asks Seth.

"I was never really based here for long," says Seth. "But if we go back out the way I came in, we should be fine. I brought these for you." He pulls a couple of items out of a bag, and hands me some glasses and a curly-haired wig. Carrick gets a cap. "To help disguise who you are."

The door to the storage room is on the other side of a

long set of metal shelves, and we follow Seth and wait while he opens it and checks to see if the coast is clear.

There's a buzzing sound behind me that's making the hairs on the back of my neck stand on end. I turn and see a small vial, glowing blue, tucked in between a range of scientific supplies. There's a tiny cork at the top holding whatever's there inside, and the vial is stuck into a wooden holder that's similar to ones I saw in Hazel's lab. Is it a demon?

Last time I was here at the SIG, having a demon with me was a useful distraction that got us out alive. I reach out and grab the vial, putting it in my jeans pocket. You never know when a demon might come in handy.

"Come on," Seth says, gesturing at us. "Coast's clear."

We follow him out into a hallway with glass windows at one end, providing a view out over the busy New York street with Central Park in the background.

Seth strides in the opposite direction, heading toward a stairwell with glass doors. We follow him, trying not to look like we're escaping. I have to keep forcing myself to slow down to a casual walk, instead of sprinting out of here like I want to. A camera is tracking our progress along the hall, but there's no sign that our presence here has alerted anyone. My wig is seriously scratchy, and I have to force myself to leave it in place.

After what feels like a million years, we reach the stairs. Seth opens the door, starting up the stairwell.

"Wait a minute. What are you doing? Shouldn't we be leaving the building?" I say.

Seth shakes his head. "This whole level is too closely monitored. We can't get out any of the exits. We have to climb to the top. We can leave from the roof. That's where I came in."

"Do the others realize this?" I ask.

"Your dad is smart. And he knows this building like the back of his hand. He'll know how to get him and Zane out. Don't worry about them. Worry about us."

Seth grabs my hand and drags me after him up the stairs. Carrick follows behind. Our rhythmic breath is the only sound that follows us up the first ten stories. I'm starting to wonder if maybe we'll be able to get out of here without a fight.

We're panting past the tenth floor when the internal siren goes off. Doors start slamming around us, and bars come down on the window next to us. Seth looks back at me and starts running up the stairs. "Two more floors," he pants. "We can do it."

My legs are burning, but I dig deeper and push myself into a run and hear Carrick doing the same just behind me. The spell web shimmers around us, but I don't pull on it just yet. My dragon strength is still enough to keep me moving up the stairs.

We're just past the eleventh floor when I hear the sound of a lift dinging and booted feet running out into a carpeted hallway. SIG agents. I can feel them through the spell web— they're all at least partial supers. The lock to the stairwell on the eleventh floor clicks, and a head pokes through. They've found us.

"Come on. We just have to beat them to the roof," says Seth. We race up the stairs, pushing hard. We pass the twelfth floor, and the elevator on that floor dings as well. They've sent guards to all the higher floors.

The door to the roof is just ahead of us. The four guards who arrived on the twelfth floor are just behind us. I turn my head to check and see them lifting their guns. They'll have an open shot at us.

I grab the tiny vial out of my pocket and, without thinking, throw it toward the guards. The vial shatters, and smoke fills the space as an enormous demon emerges out of the broken glass.

I risk a glance back, and my heart stutters in my chest. The demon is large and muscled, with flames bursting out from pockets on his skin. It looks almost exactly like the one I captured at the pawn shop. The one I used last time I was here.

Surely it can't be?

The demon roars as it spots the guards. A couple of them change their aim and shoot toward the demon, which makes it roar even louder. It takes a swipe at the closest guard, using its large meaty fist, and the guard flies through the air like he's made of feathers. The other guards back up, and the demon roars again.

"Come on, Mei, keep going," Seth urges.

But the demon is sniffing the air, like it's just noticed a roast dinner after a seven-day fast. The guards use the distraction to turn and race back through the door to the stairwell and slam the door behind them.

The demon turns and looks up the stairwell to where I'm hesitating at the door to the roof. Our eyes meet, and I see recognition flare in the demon's eyes.

It *is* the same demon.

Flames roar in its irises, and I feel its anger. It remembers just as well as I do.

The demon takes a step toward me. Then another, and then it's running up the stairs, its long legs taking them two at a time.

"Mei, come *on!*" Seth grabs at my arm and drags me through the door to the roof. My wig slides to one side, and I rip it off my head. No need for it now. Seth slams the door shut, but there's no lock, and even if there was, I don't think it would hold a demon this size.

Seth drags me away from the door, Carrick trying to stand in front of us as a first defense. He doesn't stand a chance against the demon, it's too big, too powerful.

There's only one thing I can do.

Dragging magic from the spell web around me—from the guards I can feel still cowering on level twelve, and even the demon itself—I capture it, form it into a bundle of pulsing magic that's fighting to be let free. Then I push it back against all of them, the guards and the demon. It's like an electrical charge buzzing through the bodies of the guards, and they all drop immediately, unconscious. The demon bursts through the door to the roof just as the electricity zips and zings into it, dancing over its body, making the flames burn higher. I hold my breath, not knowing if it will work on a demon. I don't know enough about them and how they work.

The demon stops, growling, but it's still conscious. I've weakened it, but my magic isn't powerful enough to knock the demon out. I let out the breath I was holding, goose bumps crawling up my skin. It's roaring in the doorway, like all I've managed to do is make it angrier.

And then suddenly my magic bursts back out of the demon, like it's pushed it out through strength of will. The electrically charged magic dances in the air above the demon for a moment, as if it can't decide what to do. Then it ricochets back at me.

It's like being hit by lightning. Pain shudders through my body, lighting up every part of me in agony. I hear Seth call out—he's still holding my hand, so he's probably received some of the charge too—but I can't do anything, my body is jerking and shaking. I can't make it stop; my body doesn't feel like my own.

The demon somehow managed to send my magic back to me, making the spell web attack me yet again. It feels worse than before, like I'm totally submerged in a vat of pain and despair. Thoughts whirl inside my head, but I can't catch hold of any of them long enough. Pain is everything inside me, the electricity adding to the needles and the fire ants. It's an agonizing cocktail that I'm being forced to drink. Is this it? Is this the moment when the spell web is going to eat me alive? I thought I had more time.

Someone lifts my arms, dragging me across the roof, and behind one of the ventilation shafts. I try to turn, to see what's happening, but I can't move.

The demon's roar is clearer now, like it's out on the roof with us.

But it's getting harder to focus. Harder to keep my eyes open. Pain surrounds me, holds me to it like a lover who just won't let go. I try to fight it, but it feels like I'm drifting further away with every second.

"I'm sorry," I whisper, before darkness falls.

20

I open my eyes, but the light is too bright. I close them again.

"She's awake." Seth's voice sounds urgent.

The demon is roaring in the background.

Where are we?

Still on the roof?

I force my eyes open. Blue sky and sunlight are all I see overhead.

"We have to get out of here," says Carrick urgently. "We can't fight a demon."

"They'll send someone up the outside of the building any minute now, too," says Seth.

I push myself up, attempting to stand. "I can fly us...."

"No offence, but I'm not getting on your back right now," says Carrick. "Seth will fly us. We were just waiting to see if you'd wake up."

"I like how sure you were that I'd wake up," I mutter.

Seth reaches down and grabs my hand, pulling me to my feet. I stumble and fall into his arms. Leaning my head against his chest, I secretly wish I could stay right there. That none of this other stuff was happening around us.

"Come on, you two," says Carrick. "No cuddling. We need to get out of here."

And just like that, my rest is over. I have to pull away from Seth and stand on my own two feet. "The demon's through the door?" I glance at a makeshift barricade they've obviously put together while I was out. Chairs, tables, metal boxes, anything they could find has been stacked around us.

"It's waiting on the other side of the barrier," says Seth, "like it thinks it has us trapped."

"Will you be able to carry Carrick without hurting him?" I ask, glancing over at the big Mountain super. When Seth turns into a phoenix, he burns with flames.

"I learned how." Seth's eyes flash with anger. "Dad found some information on phoenixes."

"What happened?" I ask. He's obviously upset. The demon roars, and this time it sounds closer.

"No time to talk about it now." Seth pulls off his T-shirt and his jeans and hands them to me. I can't help but admire him, the muscles rippling under his bronzed skin. Blazing flames appear in his eyes and then over his body, and right in front of us he transforms into a phoenix. His change is fluid and fast and magnificent. The dragon inside me growls in appreciation.

Seth gestures at me to climb onto his back, and as soon as I'm settled in between his enormous fiery wings, he grabs Carrick in his talons and takes off. Another angry roar comes from below as Seth's strong wings carry us away from the demon. I glance down and see it angrily pacing the edge of the building, like it's planning to leap after us. It's glowing blue, but it's patchy, like maybe I've taken more out of it than I realized. I grip more tightly onto Seth's back, and hope that even though it pushed my magic back into me, it's not strong enough to follow us.

I hold my breath, watching it closely. It hovers in the air but doesn't seem to be able to get any higher than a foot or so.

It doesn't leap into the air after us.

We've managed to escape.

I let out my breath in a whoosh and turn to concentrate on our flight.

We're in the air over Central Park. I've never ridden on Seth's back before—his muscles move and bunch under my legs as his wings push through the resistance of the air. The wind is flowing through my hair, the sun shining down on my face, and I feel gloriously alive. I kinda feel like lifting up my arms like Kate Winslet in *Titanic*. I manage to control the urge—I'm pretty sure I'd fall off Seth's back.

Seth's flames don't burn me—I'm a dragon and impervious to flames, but I lean over and make sure Carrick is okay below me.

He's dangling down, his eyes squeezed shut, still held tightly in Seth's talons. Aside from his obvious unease about the way he's being carried, Carrick seems fine.

I don't know what the plan is or how long Seth is going to fly us, but I do know that Carrick isn't going to last long in that position. I run my hand over the soft, leathery hide on the back of Seth's shoulders, the blue-red flames dancing over my fingers. These flames would burn a normal person, but to me they feel warm and comforting.

We continue flying over the park until we reach the southernmost edge. There's an empty clearing, and Seth brings himself down, attempting to land Carrick gently on the ground.

Carrick lands and rolls, a practiced move from his fight

training. Seth lands properly, and I crawl down off his back.

"I think I can change now," I say. "I can carry Carrick more easily than you can," Seth nods, flames burning over his long face, his black eyes burning into mine.

I grab the bag that holds our clothes from Carrick—it's a miracle he still has it after all this—and pull off my clothes. The transformation into a dragon is still painful, and I don't think it's anywhere near as beautiful as when Seth turns into a phoenix. It's aggressive and angry, a statement of intent, rather than a graceful transition.

Typical of dragons.

I gesture at Carrick with my nose, and he stuffs my clothes in the bag, and climbs on my back.

Let's get out of here, I say to Seth.

I'm right behind you.

I leap into the air, Carrick clinging tightly to my back ridges. Seth flies next to me, our wings almost touching, heading into the setting sun. This whole trip has been a bust. The only thing we learned was that there's definitely a demon plague, and that the Ravens were wrong. There is a chalice, but she's not at full strength and isn't enough to defeat the demons on her own.

In other words, the world is just as screwed as we thought. Maybe worse.

My wings beat through the air, and my thoughts go round and round.

We didn't learn anything that might save me. Or the spell web. Nothing that would help Seth. And I don't even know if Zane and Dad got out okay.

I mean, Dad's tricky. He's probably fine. But you never know.

What happened with the Ravens? I ask Seth.

They're a bunch of asshats.

Do you want to be more specific?

They tried to force me into doing a few things. Like they thought I couldn't think for myself. I pity the person who grew up in that environment when they were actually concentrating on them. I'm beginning to realize it was a lucky thing my father overlooked me all those years.

That bad, huh?

Yep.

I'm sorry I convinced you to go. I thought it'd help.

Oh, I learned enough to make it worthwhile, don't worry. They just made me real mad.

So you're ready to fly back to the compound with me?

Sure.

I hesitate. *It's good to have you back.*

I missed you too, he says with a sideways grin.

If I didn't have Carrick on my back, I'd do a loop-de-loop, or some other aerobatics, just to show him how I feel.

As it is, we fly onward. The rest of the journey is uneventful, the patterns of the land below us flowing into each other. The air currents are cool against my body, weaving through my scales and making me wish I could stay in the air forever. Up here, it's peaceful—the world is simple. Every moment is just another beat of my wings.

As the landscape thins out and becomes sand and sparse vegetation, I spot the Earthbound compound in the distance. There's smoke drifting up on the far side. I frown. That's not right. What's happening?

Carrick shouts something at me, but the wind carries it away. I look back at him, and he's pointing and yelling. Something's very wrong.

It's on fire, says Seth.

I sharpen my vision and squint toward the compound.

It's not just on fire. It's being attacked.

eth and I swoop in. I'm blazing angry.

The men down below are wearing the colors of the SIG uniforms. They have huge missile and assault weapons placed strategically around the outside walls, and they're firing inside the compound without really knowing who is inside. What if we'd decided to turn it into a school for orphans? A respite center for the elderly?

As we fly closer, I can see various fires and the craters their weapons have made, smoke rising ominously over them. While we were meeting with him in New York, the director sent his forces here to attack.

No wonder he was being such an ass. He thought he had the upper hand.

I breathe fire down over the men below me, deaf to their screams as they feel the heat of my flames. They have no right to be here. They're attacking innocent people. The director has gone too far.

Seth screeches next to me and swoops in, his enormous talons carrying off a large missile launcher. He takes it high into the air and then drops it.

The noise as it crashes to the cracked earth reverberates through me.

I breathe out more fire, and Carrick yells from my back. I think it's more of a whoop of adrenaline because he's clinging to my back as I take diving sweeps of the surrounding forces.

In the distance, another dragon roar makes me look back.

It's Zane, with my father on his back. I don't even have time to feel the relief of knowing they made it out okay.

The SIG forces are scattering below us, but there are still individuals who are self-composed enough to keep firing. Zane and Seth swoop alongside me, burning and destroying their weapons. We're lucky they don't have any of the Earthbound's devices. Bullets whizz past me, but I'm not worried—they can't penetrate dragon skin—until Carrick cries out and slumps forward over my back.

I drop down immediately, skimming the surrounding wall, and landing just outside the main building of the compound. Before I can stop him, Carrick falls off the side of my back, his body slamming into the ground.

A figure sprints out from the building.

Elena.

Her face is pale and tight, and she's running toward us like she's in the Olympics.

She reaches Carrick, turns him over, immediately checking his wound.

I transform back into my human shape, grabbing the bag that's dropped to the ground near him, and pull on my clothes.

"Is he okay?" I ask breathlessly.

"A bullet wound near his shoulder, and another one

through his side. He's losing a lot of blood." Elena's face is pinched with fear.

"Let's get him inside," I say. Carrick has saved me so many times, I've lost count. I'm not going to let him die.

She grabs his shoulders, and I've got his legs. Overhead bright flames burn as Zane and Seth continue to battle the SIG forces.

"Why didn't you go out against them?" I ask Elena.

"Carrick told me I wasn't allowed. I wasn't to take sides, or arms against anyone. I didn't want...." she trails off, gazing down at Carrick's pale form.

"He's going to be fine," I say fiercely. "I won't let anything happen to him."

I hold his legs tightly—too tightly—and we manage to get him into the building. The doors open for us, and several Mountain supers are there waiting, expecting.

I shake my head. "No. We're going to carry him." He's as heavy as an elephant, but I don't trust him to anyone else.

There's a room nearby, and we get him inside, laying his unconscious body on the tabletop. People attempt to push in around us, but Carrick's grandfather is at the door, holding them back.

"Let the dragon do her thing," he says, his voice stronger than I've heard it.

Elena hangs back, her pale face focused on Carrick's. Perhaps she's only just now realizing how much she feels for the Mountain king?

Shaking my head, I force my focus back to Carrick. I'm not going to let anything happen to him. For my sake, as well as hers.

I place one hand on his cheek, trying to feel how strong his life force is. It's weak, he's losing blood fast. I don't have much time. I pull open his shirt, ripping the buttons away.

There's blood everywhere. His chest is barely rising and falling.

Using my dragon senses, I search his body, trying to find the exact location of the bullets. My flames are burning against me, trying to get out. All my magic wants to do is turn into a dragon again. I have to force myself to go slow, to do it properly.

So many times in my life, my impatience has been why people died. I won't let it kill Carrick too.

My magic curls out from my body and dances along Carrick's skin. I let it enter his body, searching for the wounds that are so quickly taking him away. There's so much agony, so much pain. I attempt to pull back, to take some of it into me, and discover that the connection I always assumed was one way—isn't.

I can take Carrick's pain. His wounds.

Without hesitation, I drag one of his wounds onto my body through our link. The spell web contorts around me, silvery sweet and luminous, attempting to knit the shoulder wound that appears on my body back together. Blood gushes out of the wound and I stagger. Without thinking, I sink into the magic of the spell web, letting it soak me in its blazing power. When that's not enough, I start absorbing more gleaming magic from all around me, letting it fill me up. I'm taking it from Elena, Carrick's grandfather, the Mountain supers at the door, and even the SIG agents standing around on the other side of the wall. Soon it feels like I'm bathing in a glowing pool of magic that dulls the pain of the wound on my shoulder.

Then I heal the wound that's opened on my shoulder, knitting the flesh into one again.

Carrick groans and opens his eyes. "Stop it, Mei. You

can't.... Remember what...." His eyes close again, and he falls back into unconsciousness.

It doesn't matter. I wouldn't have listened to him.

The first wound has healed, the skin knitted together, leaving a raised bump. It's red and raw, but not too painful. I take a breath, holding onto the table where Carrick is lying. He's pale, covered in blood, his breathing shallow. It's not over yet. Focusing back on Carrick, I use my magic to drag his second, more serious wound onto me. As soon as the wound hits my body, my vision blurs and my legs stop being able to hold me up. I stagger to a nearby chair, grabbing at the newly formed wound at my side. Blood seeps out of my fingers, and I feel light-headed. For a second, I battle darkness, and my body tries to shut down.

"What are you doing?" asks Elena, her voice husky.

I shake my head, unable to speak. It's only through force of will that I manage to stave off unconsciousness. The wound is still oozing blood, and I feel my life force leaking away with it. In panic, I scrape more magic from everyone around me connected to the spell web—except Zane and Seth, who need their magic to continue fighting.

Once I've gathered enough power, I begin to knit the wound back together, forcing my eyes to stay open and keeping my hands clenched in my lap. It seems to take forever, like the minutes are burning themselves into my skin along with the magic.

Eventually, I let out a breath, exhaustion finally forcing me to quit. I place one hand on my side, lifting my shirt to see the damage. There's an angry-looking mottled-red scar on my skin at the side of my waist. It's only partially healed, and I have to breathe carefully to stave off the waves of pain breaking over my body.

Carrick opens his eyes. They're dark with remembered

pain and sadness. "You shouldn't have done that," he says brokenly.

I'm about to tell him to stuff his sensibilities when a familiar stinging pain starts up through my body. Needles the size of pencils are pounding into my body from all directions. The fire ants are back, and they've brought their buddies. A painful groan launches itself from my mouth, and I struggle to stay upright.

"Mei?" Elena's voice comes as if from a distance.

"I'm fine. I'll be fine. Just look after Carrick," I say, waving a hand at her.

Elena goes to Carrick, but he waves her away as well, pulling himself into a sitting position. "Mei, remember what Si taught you. The focusing tool. Do it now."

I put both my hands on my forehead, trying to stop the head-splitting pain that's reverberating inside my skull. Focus? I can't even think.

My body is suddenly too heavy to keep sitting up, and I slump sideways onto the floor, my hands only just saving my face from being smashed against the hard surface. "I...." Nothing more comes out of my mouth. It's filled with cotton wool. I feel like I'm in the middle of a hurricane, one filled with needles and angry fire ants whose only desire is to give me as much pain as possible.

It's coming at me from every direction, from inside and outside, from upside and downside. I don't know how to fight this.

All I know is, I'm going to die.

It's the last thing I think before sinking into darkness.

22

W hen I wake, I have a splitting headache and my mouth feels like sandpaper. I don't know how long it's been since I was last awake. It feels like forever.

I force my eyes open and find I'm back in my room at the Compound, under the covers of the bed. An array of concerned faces is staring down at me. Carrick and Elena, my father—wearing his arm in a sling—and Zane. Carrick's grandfather. They're all wearing different clothes, and have been cleaned up since the aerial fight. It must have been a while then.

Seth is right next to me, holding my hand. I give it a squeeze, and he leans closer and puts his hand to my cheek. "You were so still for so long. I thought...."

"I'm fine. Can't... get rid of me... that easy." I croak the words out over the gravel in my throat, and I don't think they make him feel any better.

"I saw you dive. I thought you'd been hit."

"She may as well have been," says Carrick in an angry

rush. "You didn't need to take my bullet wounds from me. I would have been fine."

"You would have died," I say, scowling at him.

"Mei, you should know better." My father's voice is equally severe. "This isn't a game anymore. You've been unconscious for almost two days. You're the spell web, which means you're responsible for more than just yourself."

"And how did you get your arm in that sling, exactly?" I ask, stung by his words. "That wasn't from sitting around, letting everyone else do the work."

"It's just a graze," he says, waving it away with his other hand. "What I'm saying is that you can't be reckless right now. You don't get to go around saving people without thinking about the consequences."

"It's who she is," says Seth quietly, staring down at me. "She's a protector, a savior. You can't change that about her."

I clutch harder at his hand.

"We can't risk her falling into the wrong hands. Or dying on us," says my father.

"I don't want to die," I croak.

"Then act like it," snaps Carrick.

"We're both still alive, aren't we?"

"That's not the point. You didn't know you'd survive."

"I do now."

Carrick's grandfather cackles. "If I'd known you were this much of a firecracker, I'd have forgiven you a lot faster for that whole spell web debacle," he says, still chortling.

"Grandfather," says Carrick severely. "You're not helping."

"Neither are you. Give the poor girl some space, all of you. Out of here now. Leave me and the phoenix alone with her." He shushes everyone, and despite some grumbling, they all leave.

"Thanks," I say, as he closes the door on them all. I push myself up to sitting against the pillows. Seth sits down next to me on the edge of the bed and I lean into him.

"You're only doing what you think is right. My grandson knows that. He's just trying to protect you, is all."

"They all are," I agree. "It's just that I was raised to protect myself."

Beside me, Seth lets out a tiny sigh.

I look up at him. "It's true. When Jeff first arrived, it was the only way he could think of to truly protect me. To basically make me into a fighting machine. That's why the protectors stopped dying."

"Because you were a dragon?"

"No, I didn't know that back then. I didn't have any dragon powers, other than an affinity for water. I just thought hard and fought hard, and learned from the masters of thinking and fighting, Jeff and Si." I wave my hand at the door. "They think I'm acting on impulse. But I'm not. I'm acting on years of thought that's been drilled into me, which has made me realize that the people I love are more important to me than anything else."

"Even if it's against what would be better for the supernatural community as a whole?" asks Seth quietly.

The words twig a memory: Si asking me the same question. Would I give up Seth if it was for the betterment of the whole community? It's too much of a coincidence. I lean away from Seth so I can see his face properly. "Did something happen while you were with the Ravens?" I ask carefully. I don't really want to know the answer, but it feels important.

"We can talk about it later," he says, looking away. "Right now, we have to get you feeling better."

"And here I thought for about five seconds that you knew me," I say.

"You're not going to let this go?" he asks with a sigh.

"No."

"While I was with the Ravens, I learned a few things."

"Like controlling your flames?"

"Yes, like that."

"What else?"

"They have some old texts, ones that talk about how to make a phoenix most useful to the supernatural community. After they've been born from the ashes."

My intuition kicks up a gear. "And what are they?" I ask suspiciously.

Seth hesitates. "It's all about how I'm supposed to be this temperamental, chaotic beast, who needs to be calmed down by those around them."

"Little bit patronizing," I say sharply. "What else?"

"They say the best way to keep a phoenix on track is to mate them with a supernatural who is calm and controlled. Someone who will help focus their powers in the right way."

Hurt blossoms in my chest. "Not a dragon, huh?" I say. I know it's not Seth's fault, but it's hard not to give in to the urge to punch him in the stomach.

He reaches out one hand, grasping my arm. "I told them to shove it. That it wasn't an option."

"But they were pretty insistent?"

"They were."

"Do you think it's true?"

"I don't care if it's true. You're the one I want to be with. You're the most important person in my life. I don't care about anyone else."

The hurt is burning a hole inside my chest. "But what if it's true? What if the only way to make this better is for you to... be with someone else?" Would I be prepared to give up Seth if that were the case? Pinpricks of light appear in my eyes. I blink them away. I don't know the answer.

"No, Mei. I refuse. We've been through too much to give up on each other like this."

The little ball of pain inside me is lessened by his words. But there's more he doesn't know. "We found something out while you were away as well." I say the words slowly, trying to figure out how this is going to change what's happening.

"What did you find out?"

I glance over at Carrick's grandfather, and immediately wish I hadn't. He's watching me with pity in his eyes.

I swallow hard. "We discovered that it's not an external force that's attacking me. It's the spell web itself. And it's probably going to consume me, sooner rather than later."

There it is. The hurt that I was looking for in Seth, to match my own. Except it doesn't make me feel better. It makes me feel like my heart is breaking into a million pieces.

"What do you mean, 'consume you'?" asks Seth carefully.

There's something stuck in my throat, and no matter how much I swallow, it won't go away. "I'm probably going... to...." I can't say the words.

"If she doesn't die because of the spell web consuming her, it will only be because she's taken her own life to save herself from the excruciating pain it will cause her as it destroys her from the inside out," says Carrick's grandfather in his gravelly voice. "We're all searching for a way to change her path, but we may not have enough time."

Seth's face is pale as he takes it in. He shakes his head. "We'll figure this out. We always do."

"What if we can't do it this time?"

"Mei, you can't give up. You never give up on other people. You never gave up on me. I won't let you give up on yourself."

"What else can we do?" I say, and I'm embarrassed by the rawness I hear in my voice.

"We talk to everyone we can. We find all the older supers for information. We hunt through the records."

"The Earthbound records still need to be decoded. They don't think they'll be able to do it in time." Again, I hesitate and look at the old Mountain super. "There's one person who could understand them."

"Who? Let's go get them."

"It's the Man in Black. The Minokawa who sided with Vincent."

The horrified look on Seth's face says it all.

"That Zane fella, he said he knew where some records might be," says Carrick's grandfather, his voice hopeful.

Seth stands up and then reaches down to drag me up next to him. "We're going to find a way out of this, Mei. I'm not going to let you go that easily. As soon as you're feeling better, I'll go get Zane and make him to take us to these records."

Even though I feel like I've just been run over by a thousand-pound steam engine, I give him a grateful grin. "Okay."

23

Zane leads us along a ridgeline, his powerful black wings skillfully dancing with the breeze. I wish I was half as graceful as he is in the air.

He's leading us to his clan's home. When Seth asked him, he didn't even hesitate, despite how difficult it is for him. For most people, 300 years is a long time past. For Zane, it feels like only a matter of months.

It's taken me a couple of days to get my strength back up to the point where I could even make the flight, and I'm still not quite at full strength, but I'm conscious of time slipping through my fingers. I need to find out if there's a way to avoid being destroyed by the spell web.

He dives around a corner and disappears. I follow more slowly and discover a large cave tucked into the cliff face with a long, high ridge out front to allow for easy access. Seth's right behind me, his fiery body bright as he dives down, landing beside me on the edge of the cave. The roof dips a bit further into the cave, and it's too dark to see anything. Zane has disappeared somewhere into the darkness.

Staying in dragon form, I duck my head low and poke my long neck into the cave proper, trying to find Zane. The low roof of the cave smoothes out into a massive cavern inside the rock. An enormous circular cliff edge opens into a deep crevice below. It's so big it takes my breath away. I shuffle my body under the dip in the roof of the cave and am rewarded when I come out into the deep cavern behind it.

How is this possible? asks Seth in awe.

I don't know, but it's amazing.

I look down over the lip of the cavern and see Zane far below, walking around slowly, still in his dragon form. There's more than enough space for his enormous body.

Should we go down there? Seth is peering down at Zane.

I think we should give him some time first. I don't know if he's been back here since he was captured.

This place is amazing. Seth's voice is filled with genuine awe. He's right. This cavern is pretty much a perfect space for creatures like us.

Zane looks up and gestures that we should join him, so we both leap off the edge of the cliff and glide down, past multiple holes in the rock walls that are presumably other rooms for the dragons who lived here.

Zane's eyes are flashing with fire, like he's only just holding himself together.

You okay? I ask.

He nods. *It's just that it's so quiet. So empty. It was never like this in my time.*

Perhaps we can make it like that again? I ask, without really meaning to. But my dragon self feels so at home here, it's hard not to fall in love with it.

Perhaps.

Zane's expression is shuttered, and I can't tell if he's annoyed that I would be so bold.

How many dragons lived here? asks Seth.

Usually around twenty to thirty families. No more than a hundred people, maybe a few more when more baby dragons were born than usual.

How did the young get around in a place like this? Before they changed? I can't imagine how anyone but supers who could fly could live here.

Internal staircases travel all up the sides of the rooms. It's fully accessible by nondragons.

I take a few steps around the sandy floor at the bottom of the cavern. There are several openings in the cave at ground level here, each one presumably going off in a different direction. They're all big enough for a dragon to walk through.

Where are the records? asks Seth.

Zane blinks, as if he's forgotten the reason we came. *This way,* he says. He leads us through one of the large open tunnels, and we follow obediently behind him.

It's not as dark as I was expecting down here. The rock has some kind of luminescent glow that keeps the tunnel light enough for a dragon to see. Plus Seth glows like a beacon wherever he is. I glance back at him. Can he turn his flames off? It'll seriously hamper his ability to sneak around if he can't.

Zane leads us into another large cavern, this one smaller than the first. There are shelves and cupboards everywhere in here, plus smaller human-sized doors. It's all a little too small for dragon size.

We should change, he says, and bends his head down to pull at the small bag attached to his back leg. It comes away immediately, and he drops it to the ground. It's an ingenious device from his time that keeps a dragon's clothes with them wherever they go. Zane begins his transformation and is soon rummaging in the bag to find his shirt and jeans.

I glance back at Seth, but he's already transforming into his human form. There's no point delaying. It's why we're here—to search the records.

"That cupboard over there should have some useful information," says Zane, pointing. His voice is bleak, but it's the only indication that this place is affecting him at all. I'm torn between going to him and trying to comfort him, and rushing over to the old, carved-wood cabinet he's indicating to search for something that might save me. Seth sees my indecision and shakes his head. Clearly he thinks I need to leave Zane alone for now.

He's probably right. Zane wouldn't thank me for being aware of his emotion, not when he's at such pains to hide it. Being here is an ordeal for him rather than an exciting field trip like it is for me.

I head to the doors Zane pointed at and open them. Inside are some very, very old books. They're all beautifully bound, individually crafted tomes in different sizes and thicknesses and patterns of gold over their colored exteriors.

I pull out one book, handling it with careful fingers. I'm almost afraid it's going to crumble at my touch, but it remains whole, and I'm able to turn over the thin paper pages, looking through the entries. It's in remarkably good condition, given how old these records are. I guess it's dry in the caverns, no dampness to cause mold or mildew.

This particular book is a record of births, deaths, and marriages. I read through it all, fascinated by the idea of so many other dragons. I'm used to small numbers, but here, in this book, there are thousands of them.

"Why is this book recording so many other dragons, not just the people who lived here?" I ask Zane.

"We were record keepers. Other dragons looked to us to keep the histories."

I put the book down on a nearby table and pull out another one. This time it's got drawings of animals in it. The next book is full of poetry so beautiful it makes my heart contract. A weird feeling is growing in my chest, and I rub it absently. This place is making me feel strange. I look around, trying to understand what it is. Is there some danger that I can't figure out?

Seth is searching through another shelf of books, opening and then closing each one as he determines what's inside it.

Zane is still wandering the room, looking around as if his memories are filling the dusty spaces. For one second, my deepest, darkest desire becomes to see exactly what he's seeing. To know what it was like to live in this place when there were so many other dragons breathing the same air, taking care of each other.

What would that have been like?

For the first time ever, I think it might just have been wonderful.

24

My eyes are almost completely crossed.

I've got a huge pile of books on the table in front of me, and none of them has been useful. At least, not in the way I need them to be.

They've been fascinating, wondrous, amazing. They've shown me a life filled with beauty and care. Of dragons simply living their lives as best they could, without the anger and aggression that so fills the history of them in our time.

What happened? Why are the stories so different? When did those terrifying murals on the Earthbound walls become the only history of the dragons that we believed in?

What really happened?

I shake my head tiredly. It's so hard to match up what I thought I knew of dragons, to the dragons who wrote these books, talking about their children, their art, or their daily lives in such a lyrical way.

Zane left to wander the rest of the dragon lair a while ago, and Seth and I have been hunting through the books ever since. We've searched through most of them and have come up completely empty.

Seth leans back and stretches, his long muscled arms reaching up over his head. "We've been down here too long. We need to take a break," he says.

I nod my agreement. As desperate as I am to find answers, there's only so much my brain can take at one time.

"Let's go outside for a bit, get some sunlight," he says.

I follow him slowly, stretching out my tired muscles. We arrive back in the main cavern and find Zane sitting on the ground, looking up.

"It used to be filled with flying dragons," he says quietly. "All the time. Kids laughing and crying, parents scolding, people talking."

I stare up through to the ledge high above us. "It must have been amazing."

"It's so quiet now. That's the hardest thing to bear," whispers Zane. "To know they were all killed by the Earthbound. It breaks my heart."

It breaks my heart too, but I don't tell him that. "We're going to head up and get some fresh air. You coming?"

He nods, and without another word strips himself down, and transforms. Seth and I do the same. The transformation into my dragon shape feels so natural now, I find it hard to remember the first time when I was so frightened and confused. The pain is almost nonexistent and is over so quickly that it's not even something I think about.

And being in my dragon form feels so good, like I'm somehow in the right place, and nothing else matters.

I spread my wings wide, and they don't even come close to touching the sides of the massive cavern. Leaping into the air, I fly upward, skimming the lip of rock at the top, and head out along the long, low cave entrance. It takes all my focus to avoid hitting the surrounding rock.

I'm pleased with myself for making it through without any problems as I emerge out into the light. My eyes are blinded for a second and I fly high, hoping that I'm not about to hit Seth or Zane.

Something screeches to one side, and I turn and squint in that direction. Is that Seth?

There are two shapes writhing in the air, one the vibrant red of Seth's phoenix shape... and the other a glowing blue.

I blink again, and recognize the demon from the SIG headquarters, clinging onto Seth in midair, its meaty fists wrapped around Seth's long phoenix neck. The demon looks much stronger than it did, its blue glow unblemished, unlike the last time I saw it.

Seth! I screech his name in my head and dive down toward them. Zane zooms over me, and hovers nearby. The demon seems to be clinging to Seth, so I'm not sure if it can fly in the air or not.

How did it find us? What's it doing here? And why is it attacking Seth?

More importantly, what can I do to hurt a demon?

I desperately try to remember the last time I met one. They don't breathe, the ice picks didn't hurt it and neither did flames. The only way I survived that time was by putting it into the tiny little bottle.

And I don't have anything like that this time.

Shit.

I hesitate, not sure how I can hurt the demon without hurting Seth. I manage to hover until I'm just next to them, trying to grab the demon away from Seth. But it's impossible, they keep turning and twisting, fighting for supremacy.

What do we do? I ask Zane.

I don't know.

The only thing I can think of is to use the spell web again, to attempt to pull more of the demon's power out of it through the web, thereby weaken it so Seth can break free.

For a second I hesitate. As soon as I use the spell web, I know what's going to happen. It's going cause excruciating pain and probably knock me out. Maybe even kill me this time.

I watch Seth struggling against the demon, his wings beating frantically as he attempts to get the upper hand. I have to decide right now.

And it's an easy decision after all. I have to try. I'd rather save Seth's life than my own—especially as I'm probably going to die soon anyway.

I land on the top of the nearby cliff. I don't even know if I can do this kind of magic in my dragon form. Closing my eyes, I reach out for my connection to the spell web. It comes to me immediately, like an eager child, wrapping me up in its glow.

Taking a deep breath, I push out along the spell web, looking for Seth and the demon.

The demon is covered in a strong pulsing section of the spell web. Without any subtlety, I use the spell web to suck out the demon's power, attempting to wrap the spell web around its body so tightly I almost strangle it as I do so.

Immediately the demon's spell web starts to dim, and the demon lets out a strangled cry, like it's in pain.

Seth grasps the waist of the demon in his talons and drags the creature away from his neck. His enormous fire-and-air wings beat majestically behind him as he hovers over a valley of rock next to the cliff where I'm swaying. Brilliant phoenix eyes glitter in the afternoon sun as he releases his talons from the demon and lets it drop down to the valley far below.

We should get out of here, leave this place before it comes back, says Seth.

I nod in agreement and look over at Zane who's still hovering near Seth. He's looking back at the cave filled with memories of his people, his expression sorrowful.

I take a step closer to the cliff's edge, planning to join the others in the sky, except my leg trips over itself, and I fall heavily onto my side. The world tilts around me and my stomach heaves. Pain launches its way up my side, and I let out a bellow. It feels like jackhammers are working on my spine, and instead of fire ants, there's a family of crocodiles with their teeth firmly wedged into my flank.

I lift my head, attempting to get to my feet again, but everything is too heavy. My wings are splayed out the back, and my feet still feel like they're tangled up. I squeeze my eyes shut and try to breathe through the pain.

Seth lands beside me. *Are you okay? Is it happening again?* His eyes are whirling, the fires inside burning brightly.

I try to open my eyes again, but they're too heavy. I can't speak any of the words I want to speak to him. Yet again, even though I fight it, darkness falls.

25

W hen I wake, I'm in the air, being awkwardly carried between Zane and Seth, each holding one end of my dragon form.

What on earth are you doing? I ask, indignant. I wriggle, and Seth's talons dig deeper into my flank. I immediately stop moving.

That demon was there for you, says Seth. *It followed you there. We had to put some distance between us.*

I don't suppose that fall killed it?

Nope. Just stunned it.

How did you know it was the same one?

It had the same pattern of flames over its body. I noticed it from last time.

I blink. He recognized the pattern of the flames? That's some serious phoenix skills right there. *How could it have followed me out here? Into the middle of nowhere?*

I don't know. But it must have. There's no way this is coincidental.

I gaze down at the scenery below us. My mind wanders for a few minutes, thinking about the implications of a demon being able to follow me around. Wherever I go. *Can you put me down? I think if you give me a few minutes, I could fly for myself.* We seem to be a long way from Zane's old home. And it's actually quite painful being carried by a phoenix and a dragon.

No longer on my bucket list, that's for sure.

Seth and Zane fly lower, near a large outcropping of rocks. They let go of me as they skim close to the ground, and I land in an awkward pile. So much for being graceful.

I push myself to my feet and stretch out my muscles. There are small, painful puncture wounds on my body where they held me in their talons and claws.

But at least I'm not dead.

Taking a step, I wobble slightly, but shake it out, determined not to give in. Seth is hovering protectively over me in the sky, while Zane loops up higher. Growing up, I never got sick. I guess I've always had a strong constitution. Until now. I'm not used to feeling weak.

Completely left in the dark about what's actually happening, yes.

Weak and shaking, no.

I swallow hard and lift my head. Gulping in a deep breath, I launch myself into the air again, this time under my own power.

The wind picks up my wings, and it feels a little like my first flight all over again. I'm out of control, wondering if I really can do this after all. And then it settles, and I'm flying steadily, using my wings to catch the wind currents and soar.

It takes a couple of hours of flying to get back to the compound. By the time we get close, I'm exhausted. We land on the rooftop, and I change immediately. My legs are like goo under me, but I manage to walk over to the wooden storage bin by the rooftop door. Our clothes are back at Zane's old home, so we grab new ones from the store Carrick has left on the roof. That's one thing I've had to come to terms with as a dragon—not to get too attached to my clothes because I'll probably end up losing them.

"You need to rest, Mei," says Seth sternly. "Every time you have one of these attacks, it makes you weaker."

"We still have a lot of work to do," I protest. "We didn't find anything useful there."

"We have time for you to rest before we do anything else."

Seth puts an arm around my waist, and he's half carrying me by the time we get down from the roof to the main floor where our rooms are. Carrick comes down the hallway as we walk down the corridor.

"How did it go?" he asks, his expression hopeful.

Seth shakes his head. "We didn't find what we were looking for."

Carrick looks me over. "You had another attack?" he asks.

I scowl at him. I don't have a better answer. The room is swaying, and I lean more heavily against Seth.

"We need to get Mei to a bed. She's about to pass out," says Seth.

I want to protest again, but the words won't form in my mouth.

It's not long before I'm floating in the comfort of my massive bed, my eyes fluttering open and shut. Seth is sitting beside me.

He takes my hand, looking down at me with a serious expression. His hair falls over his eye patch, giving his pirate face a rakish air. I want to stay awake, just to look at him. But

I can't. My body is shutting down, forcing me to sleep, to heal.

As I drift off, I hear him murmur, "I love you, Mei. I won't lose you."

I try to reply, to tell him I don't want to go anywhere, but I can't. Instead I drift off into uneasy dreams of glowing blue monsters and the spell web smothering me and everyone I love.

~

When I wake, I'm on my own.

I blink a few times, trying to get my bearings. Sunlight filters into the room through a gap in the curtains, and it feels like early morning light. I've slept the whole night? The rest of the room is the same as it was, except for a tray with sandwiches and juice on the bedside table. It looks like it's been there a while.

Flicking aside my duvet, I climb out of bed. I'm still wearing the cotton T-shirt and pants I put on yesterday. I don't feel so wobbly anymore, and everything seems to be working. The spell web is a strong pulse inside me, and my dragon magic purrs like it's ready to take on anything.

Except perhaps a demon.

I go into the bathroom and splash cold water over my face and brush my teeth. But before I do anything else, I need to find the others.

Out in the corridor, it feels strangely empty. I walk along the cold tiles, still in my bare feet, until I hear voices. Something is so strange about the atmosphere that I keep quiet, almost tip toeing along the edges of the hall.

The voices are coming from the large hall where I first met Vincent. I haven't been back in there since Carrick killed Vincent. It's covered in images of dragons being slaughtered in brutal and supposedly heroic ways by the Earthbound warriors. It gives me the creeps.

There are no guards at the slightly ajar door, so I poke my head through, my heart pounding.

Carrick and my father are talking with a stranger. He's tall, dark haired, and has the suppressed energy of a super. Through the spell web, I can tell he's a Jaguar, strong and vital, in his prime.

He looks agitated and is gesturing at my father in an aggressive way. Dad's standing there, trying to reason with him, his arm still in a sling. The stranger raises his arm threateningly, and without thinking, I race forward, ready to protect my father.

26

I slam into the stranger's side, using my momentum to get the upper hand in a situation where he has more visible body mass. I use every bit of my dragon strength to overwhelm him.

We both go sliding along the floor, and the stranger grabs at my arms, pushing me off. I roll into a fighting crouch, eyeing my enemy as he drags himself back to his feet.

Hands grab my arms from the sides, pulling me back before I can move again. Carrick has me in a firm grasp on my arm.

"Mei! Stop it! He's a friend." My father's voice is urgent.

"That's not how it looked," I insist. "His whole vibe through the spell web is agitated and violent."

"I've known Blade a long time. He's not here to hurt me."

I glare over to where Blade is watching me warily. "You sure about that?"

"Positive," says my father. He uses his one good arm to pull me up into a normal standing position. "You don't need to fly off the handle every time you meet new people, you know," he says mildly.

My hackles rise. "I don't—"

"I'm just kidding, Mei," he says with a small half smile. "Now come over here and shake hands with Blade. He's an old friend." My father puts his arm around my shoulders and gently propels me toward Blade.

"Blade, this is my daughter, Mei. Mei, this is Blade."

I reluctantly put my hand out and shake his warm one. I don't smile and neither does he.

In fact, Blade scowls at me. "The apple doesn't fall far from the tree," he says, rubbing his side. It's not a compliment.

But my father just leans his head back and laughs. "That's the nicest thing you've ever said to me. Mei's an accomplished young woman. Far more so than I ever will be."

Blade's stern green eyes size me up, as if he's trying to match what he's been told with the real me. I'm not sure he's giving me a favorable assessment.

I scowl up at him.

"Blade is here to ask for our help."

"What does he want?"

"The director figured out that Hazel helped us escape. He's locked her up in one of his high-security mountain prisons."

"Shit." Hazel, with her glasses, ripped jeans, and enthusiasm about science experiments, pops into my head. "We have to help her."

"Exactly what we were discussing," says Dad. "Blade came to us because the director's locked her up in the same facility where we rescued Zane. We've done it once. We can do it again."

I give a firm nod. No way are we going to leave Hazel locked up there. "What's the plan?"

"We haven't got that far. Blade's only just arrived."

"How long has she been locked up?"

"No more than a couple of days," growls Blade. "I came as soon as I realized."

"Security levels will still be high. They'll all be on edge," I say musingly.

"We're not going to leave her there," says Blade angrily. He turns as if he's going to leave. "I'll just—"

"Get her out on your own?" asks my father. "You'll last five minutes, Blade. Then you'll end up either locked next to her or dead. Is that what you want?"

"Of course not," says Blade, sounding aggrieved.

"Then let us help you. Mei knows what she's doing. She's been thinking on her feet since she was a kid."

A warm glow settles in my stomach.

"So what do you suggest?" Blade asks me, his expression grudging.

"I don't think they'll be expecting anyone to regroup and put together a rescue mission this quickly. Does he even know you know?"

Blade shakes his head. "No. She was supposed to be at the SIG head office for two months, and that's not up for another three weeks. They don't realize how paranoid Hazel is, how many fail-safes she set up. She's been on the run for a long time."

Something shifts inside me. That's why I like her so much. She had the same kind of upbringing as I did. "Awesome. So we have the element of surprise on our side. We also have three very capable winged operatives. So we don't need to take in any other method of travel." Last time we used jeeps to transport people, as well as dragon-back.

"If we keep the mission small, it's got more chance of succeeding," says Damien, nodding.

"So me, Seth, and Zane. We take Blade on dragon-back. We pick up Hazel and get out."

Carrick shakes his head. "I want to go as well."

"You're the Mountain king now, Carrick," says Damien.

"You need more muscle," says Carrick stubbornly.

"It's too big a risk," says Damien, shaking his head.

"I went with you to the SIG headquarters."

"And I realized very quickly how stupid that was. Your people need you right now. Your death, on top of everything else, would be too much for many of your kind."

Carrick glares at my father, but lets out a breath, giving in to the sense of what he's saying.

"Who else might be there?" I ask. "That's where we found Zane last time. Perhaps there might be other dragons?"

"It's a possibility," says my father.

"This mission is about Hazel," argues Blade, his voice a low growl. "We don't muddy the waters with other people."

"Fair enough," I say, although if we find anyone, I know what I'll be doing. "We go tonight. Fast in, fast out." Despite the energy in my voice, the thought of flying back up into the mountains is a little daunting. The last time we were there, Vincent and the Man in Black had just attacked, killing most of the people in my father's rebellion.

"I'll get the others. You'll need to plan this out with them," says Carrick. He strides off, his strong legs pounding over the tiled floor.

My father claps a hand on Blade's shoulder and leads him over to the chairs on the side wall. "We'll get her out, Blade, don't worry."

"I thought she'd be fine. I thought the director needed

her too much. That he wouldn't take action against her. He was pissed at her for helping Mei to escape." Blade eyes me up and down again, like he can't quite believe I'm a match for the director.

To be fair, I'm not sure I'm a match for him either.

"He's a smart man," says Damien. "He doesn't usually do things out of anger. So he's either got some other purpose in mind by locking Hazel up, which means this is a trap, or the situation with the demons is far worse than we thought, and he's closer to the edge than any one realizes."

"I'm not sure which of those options is better," I say.

"Either way, we have to get Hazel out of there." Blade glances at me again and then back at my father. "Damien, may I have a word in private?"

I let out an impatient breath. "If this is about not trusting me to run this mission, save it. I'm the best option you have, aside from my father, who is clearly out of action," I say, gesturing at my father's wounded arm.

"I wish I could go with you, Blade. But I'm not over-stating things. Mei's smart. Together, you'll get Hazel out of there."

Blade looks at me, his expression mulish. He really doesn't approve of me for some reason.

It's lucky for him I don't need his approval. And that I'm not working on my own. Annoyingly, when Zane and Seth come in not long after, Blade relaxes slightly. He stands up and shakes hands with the older dragon and obviously powerful phoenix shifter. No matter that I have more magic flowing through my veins than both of them put together. No matter that I was trained since I was a kid for this kind of situation. I manage to hold my hands steady, to avoid clenching them like I really want to. Sometimes I wish I was tall, muscled, and mean-looking. Intimidating on the outside as well as the inside.

It's better for everyone to underestimate you, Mei. They'll learn soon enough. Jeff's voice is just a tiny whisper inside my head these days, but his words hit home.

I don't need Blade's approval.

I just need to get Hazel the hell out of there.

27

The night is black.

The sliver of a moon that was visible earlier has been covered by clouds. Luckily none of us need the light to fly through the mountains. Seth is beside me, his flames dimmed to a fiery glow that's heating up the night sky, and Zane is on the other side, carrying Blade.

The mission has been planned down to the tiniest detail, the others enthusiastically joining in once they'd been told what we were planning. Zane and Seth both knew better than to offer any opinions about me not leading, and it seemed to calm Blade down when he saw how they both interacted with me.

Not that it matters.

If we all do our part, Hazel will be free in no time.

I swoop in low toward the prison, which is sitting in the lee of the mountains below us. Guards line the high walls, machine guns at the ready. They're clearly prepared for anything.

I don't know if they're waiting on us, or if it's just para-

noia on the part of whoever is running this place. Either
way, it doesn't matter.

I open my mouth and blaze out a line of dragon fire
along the wall, just missing the guards. They all turn toward
me as one, and Zane, under cover of the distraction, flies in
on the other end of the building with Blade.

Seth roars and swoops in, grabbing a guard in his talons
and carrying the struggling man away, dropping him on a
cliffside ledge not far away. As he keeps grabbing them,
guard after guard, I'm flying up and down the wall, using my
flames to keep the other guards occupied. They're yelling
and screaming orders at each other, running around like
they're trying to figure out what to do and have no idea what
that might be.

A few of the more levelheaded guards are actually
shooting at me, but my dragon underbelly is too tough for
their bullets. Even the thin leathery skin on my wings is
impervious. It's probably something to do with the magic of
the spell web, or some kind of protective magic inside me,
but I'll take it, whatever the reason.

I send a fiery warning down to one guard who's surprisingly accurate with his shots. I don't want to find out the
hard way that some part of me isn't as impervious as I
thought. The guard dives down into the stairwell to save
himself, leaving his automatic weapon on the ground. I
flame it again, just to be sure it can't be used on me.

Seth has all but a couple of the guards now sitting on
inaccessible ledges around the prison, and I pick up one of
the last two, carrying him to the nearest unoccupied ledge.

I turn back to the wall to find another two men have
appeared via the main staircase.

One is a squat man with a mean expression and a pot

belly. The second is a tall man, wearing black. My stomach lurches as I recognize the second man.

It's the Man in Black. He's here, I say to Seth. Rage fills my vision.

He has some nasty friends.

For a moment, I hesitate. I'm not afraid of the SIG guards, but the Man in Black is a whole other matter. He's a minokawa, said to have all sorts of magical abilities, including enough magic to hold the King of the Mountain supers in thrall. He killed Liling right in front of me, and then he helped Vincent find our mountain stronghold where they killed more than 250 people. He's not at the top of my hit list, but he's close. Only problem is that I don't really know what his powers are, and I'm not certain I could kill him in a fight.

But then, what does it matter? At the moment, my life is pretty much hanging in the balance anyway. I swoop down toward the two men and send a burst of flames in their direction.

As one, the two men step back, out of the line of my fire. Neither one seems particularly concerned about it.

And then a third man appears, this time carrying a small metal box. It's one I recognize straight away. It's one of the Earthbound's contraptions, designed to steal the magic from a dragon.

Shit.

I roar and, without thinking, dive back down for them, aiming all my energy at the terrifying box in front of me. Those things caused the deaths of thousands of dragons, wiping their magic so the Earthbound could slaughter them.

The man with the box backs up, but he does something

on the side that seems to turn it on. I don't know how long before it starts working, but I don't plan to give it a chance.

The claws on my back legs are strong, and I reach down, attempting to grab at the box with them—or at least to scratch it so badly it breaks.

I miss, swooping alongside the wall and over into the prison courtyard. A high-pitched screech starts up, and I immediately feel myself changing back into my human form. I resist with everything I have, but it's no use. The machine is stronger than I am.

One minute I'm flying low to the ground, the next I'm rolling over the paving stones inside the compound in my human form. I stand up, turning immediately, preparing to fight, even if I have to do it naked. Scratches from the rough stones are stinging over my whole body, and my ears are ringing from the forced change back to my human form.

A streak of black runs across the courtyard, and up the stairs toward the Minokawa.

Blade.

I turn and check in the direction he came from, and see Zane and Hazel running out of the main prison building. I'm itching to follow Blade, but first I have to make sure Hazel is okay.

"Little chilly to be naked," says Hazel, looking me up and down. She pulls off her lab coat, which she's still wearing for some reason, and hands it to me.

"Thanks," I say as I pull it on. It's a little dirty, but it *is* kinda cold out here. I didn't bring a change of clothes like Zane, because I wasn't planning to change into human form.

"How do we get out of here now with the machine keeping us human?" asks Zane. His expression is pained, and I remember that Tarsal was affected by the machine's noises far more than I was. Something protected me. What's different between us?

He's older, sure. But that should just be about experience. And then it hits me.

The spell web.

I take a breath and then pull the spell web more securely over the three of us and add an extra layer of protection over Zane. I try not to use too much of its magic, desperately hoping I won't trigger an attack. Immediately Zane's eyes are clearer, and he frowns over at me.

"What did you do?"

"Just a little added protection." I glance up toward the parapet where Blade disappeared. Anger and fear are battling for supremacy in my chest. Rage wins. "We need to help Blade. The minokawa is a merciless killer."

Before I can say anything else, Hazel races toward the stairwell without a second thought. We run after her, with me wrapping us in the spell web for protection. Anything to give us an advantage.

We get to the top of the stairwell and emerge on the prison wall to find Blade and the Man in Black locked in a vicious battle. They're so closely matched, neither one can get an upper hand. My hand clenches, and I take a step forward, wanting to intervene, to find a way to kill the man in black for what he's done to the people I love.

My foot hits something on the ground, and I look down. The other two guards are unconscious on the ground in front of me. It obviously didn't take much for Blade to know them out. Maybe he's more formidable than I gave him credit for.

"How can we help him?" I ask Hazel. I've realized don't know Blade's capabilities. Maybe me leaping into the fight would just hamper what Blade can do, and maybe help the man in black win. I have to be careful.

"He's strong. And powerful. Used to fighting demons. Leave him to figure this out," says Hazel confidently. Despite her words, her eyes are scared, and her whole body is tense. I move around to one side of the fight between the two powerful supers. As soon as I see an opportunity, I'm going to take it. The man in black isn't going to escape this time.

Blade lands a punch that sends the man in black sprawling across the floor. Instead of getting up and returning to the fight, he turns, magic surging as he morphs into his black flying lizard-bird form. Long metal feathers emerge, looking sharp and deadly in the lights of the prison. His wings are jagged black reminders of what he can do. Memories of blood and screams fill my head, and I hesitate.

He opens his serrated beak and gives a terrible screech, the walls shuddering around us. Blade takes a step forward, clearly intending to give chase.

Hazel lets out a tiny horrified noise, like she wants to stop Blade, but before she can move, the man in Black leaps into the air, and with a powerful beat of his enormous black wings, is out of our reach.

He disappears before any of us can even move to stop him.

28

I blink, realizing we just let him go. The man responsible for Liling's death and the death of so many of my friends. I feel sick to my stomach. I should have done something more. I glance at Hazel, and she has a similar expression on her face to mine.

What did the man in black do to her? She's been trapped in this place with him for the last three days. I can't even imagine.

Hazel's expression is filled with agony, like she's just watched her family being killed in front of her. Rage returns as I realize she must have suffered something terrible at the hands of the man in black. What did he do to her, that made her lust for his death so badly?

"Everyone okay?" Hazel asks in a shaky voice as she runs to Blade, touching his chest as if checking for wounds. It's clear she's not really asking the rest of us. I shake out my arms and legs, trying to get rid of the adrenaline that's flowing through my system, making me feel hyper-alive. Looking around, I try to assess what's left of the situation. The guards have either been knocked out or run from us.

Blade lets Hazel check for wounds for a few seconds more before catching both hands in one of his. "I'm fine, Hazel."

Hazel kisses him on the lips, holding him close. It's a private moment, but I can't help watching. There's something compelling about the two of them together. He whispers something in her ear, meant only for her. Even though I could have listened with my dragon hearing, I hum under my breath, blocking it out.

Hazel visibly relaxes, and kisses him on the chin. Whatever he told her, she's lost that expression of despair, and something in my chest eases.

"We need to get out of here," says Blade roughly, looking around. He's holding Hazel's hand tightly in his.

Hazel turns to look at the metal box on the wall. "Is this one of the Earthbound contraptions?" she asks.

I glance down at the box in surprise. The effects of the box aren't as strong on me now that I've got the spell web inside me. I managed to take away some of the pain for both Zane and I. But it's still blocking my ability to turn into a dragon, and I feel my magic swirling inside me, fighting against the block. It's like there's an itch I can't scratch over the whole of my body.

"Yes, and we'd love it if you could please turn it off," says Zane tersely.

I glance at him. He's pale and looks, despite my efforts, like he's in pain.

Hazel crouches down and fiddles with the box for a moment, and then suddenly the pressure that's been causing the blood to churn inside my body stops.

I let out a relieved breath.

"Where'd they get one of those?" I ask. The boxes keep popping up at the most annoying times. We need to find a way to either fight back against their power, or destroy them all completely.

"Where do you think?" says Zane, his expression hard. "From your favorite Earthbound leader."

Seth's brightly flaming form appears in the sky above us. I can't help the way my heart leaps in my chest at the sight of him. He's magnificent.

We need to keep moving, he says impatiently. *There are more of them coming.*

And apparently grumpy. To be fair to us, we didn't plan on having to defend ourselves from anyone other than a few supernatural guards.

But he's right, we need to get out of here, right now.

I'm nodding the affirmative, looking around for a good place to shift, when a sizzling, popping sound distracts us all. A blue glow appears at the far end of the wall, forming quickly into the powerful shape of a demon. It snarls, looks around and then spots me. It walks toward us along the top of the prison's wall, the smell of ash and brimstone crawling before it. But it's not just any large demon.

It's *my* large demon.

"How the hell did it find us again?" I ask incredulously. My hands clench into fists, and I turn to fully face the demon that's striding toward us. It's still glowing blue, smoke billowing around it like some kind of see-through cape. Its black eyes are trained on me, and if looks could kill, I'd be dead. I steel myself to fight the demon the only way I know how—by using the spell web, and getting myself knocked out.

"You recognize it?" asks Hazel curiously, moving to stand next to me. "I've never met anyone besides myself, and sometimes Blade, who can do that."

"It's one that I fought and then locked in a bottle a while

back. I set it free, only for it to be captured by the SIG again. I think it's holding a grudge against me." I take a step toward the demon, preparing to fight it. It's started to solidify into its more human form, little pustules of fire bursting out from its skin. It clenches its meaty fists and lifts them slightly, as if readying itself for the coming fight. Last time the spell web didn't work completely, but it did slow it down a little, perhaps—

"A grudge? Interesting." Hazel stands up, her glasses lit with the reflection of the demon advancing on us.

I register the fact that instead of moving away, she's moved forward alongside me.

"You need to get out of here," I say, glancing back at Blade and then Hazel. "He's a pretty strong demon. I'm not sure—"

"Don't worry, Mei. You can leave this one to me," says Hazel softly. She walks past me until she's standing a couple yards from the demon. It growls at her, showing enormous teeth that seem too big for its mouth. The sense of menace grows until the air is thick with it.

I move forward again, standing just in front of Hazel, my attention focused on the demon. I'm frantically trying to remember how I've beaten it before, but my thoughts are too scrambled. "Seriously, Hazel. You need to step back," I say, giving her a quick glance. "This demon's dangerous. I can slow it down, give us enough time to get out of here. But I can't do that if I'm worried about you getting in the way."

"You're kind of in *my* way," says Hazel softly. She puts one hand on my arm, and draws me behind her. I'm so surprised by her words and the glowing power on her face that I let her do it.

But still I hesitate. Surely she can't go up against a demon this size? "Is she going to be okay?" I glance back at

Blade. He's usually the king of overprotectiveness when it comes to Hazel, but right now he's standing back behind us, his arms crossed over his chest and eyes fixed on Hazel with smug satisfaction.

"She's going to kick its butt," he says.

Looking back at Hazel, I try to see what he's seeing. She doesn't seem like she could take on much of anything, let alone an enormous salivating demon. But then again, didn't Blade have the same thoughts about me? I'm underestimating her just like Blade did to me, and I know how crummy that feels.

I finally take another step back, giving Hazel room to do her thing.

But I also wrap the spell web close to me, ready to leap forward and help if I think she needs it. No sense in being completely unprepared.

A humming rises up out of the darkness, and I peer around, looking for the source. The sound increases, becomes a song, and I realize it's Hazel. The demon in front of her is looking less certain, its face starting to blur.

The notes from Hazel keep going up the scale, until they're ridiculously high-pitched. I'm not sure a human would be able to hear them anymore.

The demon is looking panicky, like it's trying to escape but can't. Hazel's hair is being blown up around her by a wind that's not affecting anyone else.

The demon changes again, becoming a glowing blue shape. Tendrils of the mist try to flee off into the mountains, but Hazel opens her mouth wide, and suddenly the demon is being sucked toward her.

I take a step forward, still not convinced that Hazel knows what she's doing, but a strong hand on my arm still me. I glance back at Blade, and he shakes his head once.

"Hazel can handle it," he says.

I step back again, trying to overcome the desperate need inside me to fight the demon alongside Hazel. My dragon's only goal is to transform, to dominate the demon.

Instead I clench my fists and force myself to stand still as Hazel battles it for us.

29

The demon is trying to pull itself away from Hazel.

It's frantically looking from side to side and scrabbling for purchase on the wall behind it, but the suction is too strong.

The demon's shape stretches and elongates as it attempts to avoid whatever she has planned for it. There's a discordant buzzing in the air, and invisible sparks of power make my skin prickle as the two opposing forces smash up against each other, creating a kind of magical friction.

The feet hit Hazel's body first, lighting her face with a reflected blue glow as it gets absorbed into her body. The demon fights her every step of the way, snarling and pulling itself into strange shapes like some kind of Salvador Dali sculpture gone wrong. I hold my breath, watching with morbid fascination as the creature—which only moments before seemed too powerful to subdue—crinkles down into increasingly smaller dimensions. The air ripples around us like an echo of the demon's formerly magnificent form.

Soon it's just a weird blue lump sticking out from her

stomach. Seconds later, the demon has been completely absorbed into Hazel.

Part of me is expecting her to start glowing blue, or for the demon to take over her body and attack the rest of us again. I keep my stance active and ready for whatever's going to happen. But Hazel just turns and smiles, her face pale, dark smudges under her eyes the only indication that absorbing the demon was harder than it looked.

"Are you okay?" I say cautiously. I still can't believe she absorbed the demon right in front of us.

"Sure, I'm good," says Hazel. "Demons are my thing."

I look from Hazel to Blade, my brain trying to catch up with what we just witnessed. "How is that even possible?"

Hazel shrugs. "Not so long ago, I would have sworn that people who could change into dragons were impossible."

I nod. Fair point. It's not like we don't all have our own strengths. But to take on a demon that size so easily...

In the sky above us Seth gives a screech, reminding me that we're in a hurry. I give my head a quick shake to clear it. "Okay, so where to now?" I ask Blade. He'd mentioned a hideaway but didn't give specifics.

"Just head for the California coast. I'll guide you from there," says Blade.

"And you're sure you're all good?" I ask Hazel again.

"Let's just get out of here." She looks pointedly at me and Zane.

I glance over at Zane and he shrugs. She's more hard-core than I'd given her credit for. I pull off her lab coat and make the transformation into a dragon. As usual, I feel pinpricks of pain as my bones morph and change into something much, much larger, but the joy and pleasure of my dragon form erases any memory of the transformation.

Are you ready? I ask Seth as Hazel climbs onto my back.

I'm surprised that Blade is willing to leave her side, but it's far more sensible to have one person per dragon. It seems he's not all just emotion and anger. In fact he seems much calmer now that we have Hazel back with us.

We need to get out of here. There are reinforcements coming, is Seth's only answer.

I leap into the air, making sure I do it smoothly enough that Hazel won't fall off on her first dragon ride. Zane and Blade make it into the air beside us, and we swoop off through the mountains. A siren erupts into the dark night behind us. I beat my wings faster, eager to fly away now that we have the person we came for.

The flight to California seems to take forever. We fly low over the terrain, trying to keep out of the more populated areas. My wings are aching long before we see the distant sparkle of the moon on the ocean.

Blade points up the coast, and we soar through the dark sky, the stars our only company.

He leads us to a mansion perched on a high cliff, looking out over the Pacific Ocean. There's nothing except trees and forest for miles on either side. Clearly Blade is wealthier than I gave him credit for.

The sun is just rising over the water as we land on an enormous perfectly mowed lawn. Hazel and Blade climb down from Zane and me, stretching stiffly when they reach the ground. Given how tired I am, I can only imagine what they're feeling. I turn my long neck and watch as they walk across the lawn, Hazel a little wobbly until Blade puts his arm around her.

Closing my eyes, I begin the transformation into my human shape, my bones morphing magically until I'm a mere fraction of my previous size. I feel heavier in this form than I was as a dragon and everything aches, most especially my arms, which feel like I've just done a press-up marathon. Seth has already changed, and hands me the clothes he stashed for us. I'm so tired I only spare a fleeting glance at his golden-skinned bare chest before I drag on my shirt and jeans. Zane strides off ahead of us, his dark hair whipping in the cold night air.

Seth comes up beside me and grabs my hand, squeezing it. I smile up at him as we walk across the lawns in Zane's wake. Blade's place is so amazing I feel like I'm gawking round like a tourist. The house has floor-to-ceiling windows and doors along the front, and it's two stories high, so the views up top must be even better than they are down here. There's a massive kidney-shaped pool out the front with a waterfall and a hot tub off to one side.

It's utter luxury.

Inside, it's minimalistic with a large cream living room set facing the sun out the windows and cream rugs over the pale-tiled floor. The only thing that seems out of place is a weird sculpture made of metal scrap parts that looks a little like Blade. If I had to guess, I'd say it belonged to Hazel.

Hazel is smashed up against Blade's side on the sofa, obviously pleased to be home. She's not paying any attention to the fancy surroundings. There's a rather large possibility she doesn't even notice them.

"I need to shower and get out of these clothes," Hazel says to us, as she reluctantly stands up, still holding onto Blade's hand. "Make yourself at home. Blade is a terrible host. He'll probably forget to even offer you a drink."

Blade glares up at her from his position on the couch, but he pulls her back down into his lap at the same time and wraps his arms around her, as if he can't bear to have her away from his side. He leans in and their lips meet in a tender kiss that seems so intimate, I have to look away.

Seth clears his throat, and they break away, Hazel looking at us guiltily over her shoulder.

"While I'm gone, Blade will take you to your rooms. You can rest. Later, I'll take you down to my lab. Blade had it built for me," she says with a fond glance at Blade. "We can discuss the demon plague and how you can help me with it."

She leaves the room calmly as if she hasn't just dropped a bombshell.

azel's basement lab is far more high tech than the name implies.

Brightly lit stainless steel bench tops dominate the enormous space, with high tech machinery everywhere, and cabinets and coolers filled with presumably useful equipment. I follow Hazel into the room, Seth just behind me. Zane is upstairs with Blade, looking over the property.

"This is where I like to work. Now I've quit my job at the SIG, I can be here more often."

"When did you quit your job?" I ask curiously. Was that why they arrested her?

"When they put me in prison," says Hazel with a smart-ass grin.

I can't help my quick burst of laughter. "Maybe you should have considered doing it a bit earlier?"

"Maybe," answers Hazel, her nose already buried in a cabinet to one side of the room. She pokes her head out again. "I'd like to check your vitals. Take some details for further study of different types of supernaturals. Is that okay?"

"You can take whatever you like from me, but first you have to tell us what you know about the demon plague. Is it really as bad as the Ravens think it will be?"

"I suppose that depends on what the Ravens are expecting?"

Seth steps forward. "They're expecting the demon plague to be so bad, maybe the humans and the other supernaturals won't survive it."

Hazel raises her eyebrows in surprise. "That's an awfully dark estimation of things. No, I don't think it will be that bad."

"Then how bad?"

"The demons are strong in numbers. In some areas, it's getting difficult to keep them under control. I suspect this is because of a man named Connor McKenzie. He's part super, son of a siren." She mutters something under her breath.

"What's he doing?" I ask, trying to keep her focused.

"He's drawing older demons in, creating situations for the perfect formation of new demons. He believes he can control them, use their magic for energy. He believes he can make money from them, essentially."

"But that's just crazy," I say.

"Not entirely crazy. It *is* possible to use the energy from a demon to create a power grid we can use. It's just that it's very unstable, and extremely dangerous. He doesn't have all the facts and refuses to listen to me."

"You've talked to him?"

"He's working with the Director. Connor has convinced him that he can create this kind of energy safely."

I lean against the nearest counter. This is why the Director was so smug. He's not really that interested in me or the spell web. He's got other plans. "Then why did he attack the Earthbound compound?"

"Connor's convinced there's information at the compound that will help them set up the demon power grid. Apparently at one point the Earthbound were experimenting with using demons to control the dragons."

The breath leaves my body in a rush. "This changes everything. I thought the Director was after me. Trying to control me."

"We all did," says Seth, catching hold of my hand. "It's a relief that he's not focused on you."

"Could he use the demons to do more than create energy? Could he use their power to compete with the spell web? To bring it down? Or hide from it?"

"Theoretically, anything is possible. They'd just have to run tests. But remember, it's highly unstable. It's just as likely they'd kill us all off."

Hazel says the words with such a matter-of-fact tone, I don't immediately realize she's talking about the annihilation of the human and super races.

"Is that a possibility?"

"A high possibility. They don't realize what they're dealing with."

"Didn't you say you told them?" asks Seth.

Hazel shrugs. "They think they know better than me. Or maybe they just don't care? The possibility of wealth can sometimes blind people to the truth."

"So what can we do to stop them?"

"I'm working on a few things. That's why I agreed to go to the SIG headquarters. The director has been trying to get me into his demon lab for a long time, so he leapt at the chance when I said I'd go. I used it as an opportunity to get information on their plans."

"And what did you find out?"

"That they're both as nutty as a fruitcake. They have no other system to help them than the one I developed for them in the early days before I realized what they were doing. It's unstable, dangerous, and I never managed to get a demon to stay inside it for more than ten days. They're just ignoring all that." Hazel strikes her open palm on her leg, making a loud slapping sound that echoes around the room and makes me jump. "They're idiots."

"Can't you control the demons?" I ask. "Maybe we could just... I don't know... corral them or something?"

Hazel shakes her head. "I can control a few of them. Maybe even as many as twenty at one time. But not hundreds by myself. I'm working on ways to amplify that, but—"

"Can we sabotage the system you built?" I say, determined to find a solution. "We could try to get into wherever it's being kept and break it."

"Like you did with the spell web?" asks Hazel mildly, her eyebrows raised. She clearly wasn't a fan of being without the spell web.

"It wasn't on purpose," I say defensively.

"Exactly my point. Rushing in and attempting to break a system we're not completely sure about is not the best option."

"Then what is?"

"Whatever we do, it needs to be something that will maintain the status quo, that keeps the spell web in place so it hides the demons from the humans."

"There might not be much we can do about that," I say.

"What do you mean?" Hazel eyes me sharply.

"The spell web. Putting it inside me turns out to have been a bad idea." I take a breath, trying not to let the fear and doubt crawl their way up inside my body. "It's devouring me, piece by piece. When I die, so will the spell web. We'll go back to the humans being able to see the supers. Back to square one with our problems. Except I won't be here to stop it a second time." I end on a whisper, and Seth puts one arm around my shoulders. I lean into him, letting him give me the comfort I need. It never gets easy to say that I'm going to die.

Hazel is watching me carefully. "I could run some tests...," she says hesitantly. "I don't quite understand how the spell web works, but if you want me to see what I can find out, I'm down with that."

I look up, and move away from Seth's embrace. "You could do that?" I ask.

Hazel nods. "Of course. I can't guarantee what I'd find, but I can do the tests."

It would be more information than we have now. Maybe it could lead us to a solution. "That would be amazing. Test away."

"No time like the present," says Hazel, gesturing at us to join her in the sea of scientific devices near a padded chair and a padded patient table at the far side of the lab.

"First you need to answer some questions about how it works," says Hazel as she fusses around with various machines. "We can talk while I set up a few of the devices to check your vitals. I've been testing Blade, just to see how supers are different from humans."

Hazel leads me over to a chair where she's set up all kinds of monitors. "Is that an ECG machine?" I ask.

"Sure is." She places the small sticky squares over my body, gesturing to Seth to move back and away from the chair. He stands to one side with his arms crossed, watching with fiery eyes. He's about as comfortable with this as I feel.

But if I want answers, this is important.

"The Ravens said... they said there were no chalices left," says Seth. "How come they didn't know about you?"

"*I* didn't know about me," says Hazel. "I was brought up in a tiny, backwater community in the middle of nowhere. I didn't know I was a chalice until very recently." Hazel glances upward as if she knows exactly where Blade is. "Until Blade found me."

"How do you know how to do all this stuff?" I ask, gesturing around at the weird gadgets and machines surrounding me.

"I taught myself. My parents... were killed by a demon. And so was my best friend."

"I'm so sorry," I say, wishing I could offer her something more.

"Thanks. I didn't know it was demons at the time. I didn't know anything about the supernatural. I just thought it was scary glowing monsters. I was determined to find out what had caused their deaths. So I kind of went on this quest."

"Quest? Like a knight of the round table?"

Hazel gives a snort of laughter. "More like Scooby-Doo and Shaggy. I learned how to keep under the radar, and I figured out what I needed to know to get answers."

"And did you get your answers?"

"I'm still working on it," says Hazel absently, staring down at a machine.

"I can't believe you did all that on your own," I say. "And that you had no idea about supers."

"It's funny to remember it now. I don't know how my parents managed to keep me away from anything relating to the supernatural, but they did. I honestly had no clue."

"I guess we're all so used to hiding in the shadows; you have to know what to look for."

"Maybe." Hazel is watching the little needle on the ECG machine bounce up and down. She grabs a strange headset with wires coming out of it. "This is going to measure your brain waves."

She places it on my head and tightens the straps so it can't fall off.

Another set of needles on paper start to jump around on the machine next to the ECG. "What's it telling you?" I ask curiously.

"That you're super healthy. That your brain has a lot going on inside it."

"Good to know. I think."

"It's good. Your brain waves are similar—"

The ringing of a mobile phone interrupts Hazel's flow. Seth reaches into his back pocket and pulls out his phone. "It's my father," he says grimly. He goes to put it back in his pocket.

"Answer it," I say firmly. "It could be important."

He hesitates. "Fine." He presses the button. "What do you want?" he asks grimly, as he turns to walk to the other side of the room.

"I take it they don't get along?" asks Hazel curiously.

"Not really. Ravens are a special breed."

"But Seth's not a Raven...?"

"He grew up a Raven. Ravens have the phoenix gene inside them. When times are hard, the phoenix appears to help save the world. Or so they say."

Hazel's eyes widen, and she looks over at Seth with renewed interest. "I should definitely check his vitals too," she says.

"I'm sure he'd be happy to do that," I say, trying to suppress a grin at her obvious enthusiasm for the tests.

Seth walks back to us, and we both watch as he approaches, his face stormy. "He's asking me to come back. He says it's urgent, something to do with my brother, but he won't tell me why on the phone. Says it could be hacked."

"Do you believe him?"

"He seemed upset." Seth's expression is grim, his eyes flashing annoyance.

"What if Mike's in trouble? You should check it out. If he's lying, or playing games, come straight back here. And tell him he just cried wolf one too many times."

Seth lets out a breath. "I want to tell him to go jump."

"I know. I get it," I say, wishing I wasn't still hooked up to two different machines. I want to crush him against me, to hold him tight. "But right now, we need the Ravens. And we're living in dangerous times. It really could be something important."

He comes over to me and leans down to kiss my forehead. "You are, strangely, the voice of reason in this instance," he says. "I'm gonna leave now, while you and Hazel are occupied with your testing. I'll be back in a few days."

"Take care," I whisper, grabbing his hand and squeezing it tight.

"Of course," he replies. "Always."

31

"So if the spell web is eating at you, what part of you is it eating?" asks Hazel. She's standing next to me, fiddling with the dials on the ECG, which is still recording my heart beats. "Your soul? Your flesh? Your heart?"

I pause and think about it. "My magic, I suppose. Carrick's grandfather said it had done the same thing with other supernaturals when the Earthbound were testing it." I try not to move too much or breathe too loudly. I'm not sure if that's what she wants of me, but I'm not used to this amount of medical attention.

"Which is why he thinks it's going to do the same to you?"

"Yep."

"Where did he get his information? Was it documented?"

"It was handed down verbally."

Hazel raises her eyebrows. "That's not very scientific."

"It's how the Mountain supers do it. They know their histories. They don't do research."

"So there's a very large possibility they've got it wrong. Or they've misunderstood something. Or there's a way out of this," says Hazel. "That's positive."

"Don't get my hopes up," I warn. "I don't want to find out later they were bang-on accurate."

"Okay. Fair enough. So what does it feel like to have the spell web inside you?"

I hesitate, trying to figure out the best way to answer her question. "When I swallowed the power of the spell web, it felt like it was going to break me into a million pieces. Like I was going to explode from the pressure of too much magic pulsing inside me. There was too much energy, too much magic for one person to control. And then I guess my magic figured it out, and everything settled down." I pause, considering the rest of my answer. "I see further and more clearly, hear better, am stronger and faster, even more so than when I was just a dragon. I can pull on the spell web around me and use its magic to do what I want in my environment. Except at the moment, every time I pull on it too much, I have one of these attacks. And I still can't beat a demon," I say, making a face.

"Because they're not the same as humans and supers. They live on a different plane of existence. They don't die like we do. They just go back to where they're supposed to be."

"Do they have more energy than humans and supers?"

"Essentially they're made up of energy. But it's not stable. It's a chaotic, angry kind of energy that would kill you as soon as look at you."

"What's the deal with the one that was following me around? I didn't think they could do things like that."

Hazel frowns. "They don't usually. But it must have

bonded to you somehow. You made an impression on it."
She hesitates. "What did you do to it, precisely?"

I scrunch my eyes up, remembering back to the pawn
shop where I fought the demon. "I let it out of a bottle,
watched it kill the super who put it there, and then
managed to survive when it came after me by putting it into
another bottle. Then I carried it around with me for a while.
I figure that's why it's angry."

"If you carried it with you, that's probably enough. A
demon that size, it's been around a long time. It carries a lot
of anger."

I shudder, remembering the demon and how scary it
was the first time I met it. "I don't think I ever said thank you
for saving me. I don't know how I would have stopped it
from trying to kill me."

"No problem. You saved me as well, don't forget."

"Let's say we're even," I say with a grin.

Hazel nods and readjusts one of the sensors on the band
around my head. "So let's go through what we know. How
many attacks have you had?"

"Three or four?"

"And what's happening when they occur? What are you
doing?"

"It's when I'm drawing on the spell web. The last couple
of times the only reason I used it was because we had no
other option—it was my last resort. I knew it would aggra-
vate things and probably cause an attack, but I had to do it
anyway."

"So, highly emotional or charged situations when you
pull on the magic of the spell web." Hazel is nodding. "This
is something we can test. We can hook you up to the monitors and get you to use the spell web like you have been.
Then watch exactly what happens."

"I guess," I say reluctantly. "Do you want to do it now?"

Hazel hesitates. "Let's just keep monitoring you for now. I don't want to make it worse for you, and you're probably tired from rescuing me. You need to get your strength up again."

I nod, relieved. "The attacks... they're not that much fun. In fact they hurt like a bitch. So if you want to do it, okay. But I can't do it multiple times. You'll only get one shot at it."

"Understood. So let's make it optimal."

"Have you found anything out about me based on all these monitors?" I gesture toward the notepad she's been using.

"Well, I can see clear differences between you and an ordinary human. And I've also found a few ways you're different from a super like Blade."

"Have other supers done this kind of research before?" I ask curiously.

"I guess maybe the SIG? But Blade says most of their operatives are only part supernatural, and they're not focused on research so much as keeping the peace between humans and supers."

"The Earthbound seem to have done a whole heap of research in their time. But I don't think they were that interested in the betterment of the supernatural community." I can't help the bitterness that soaks my voice.

If she notices, Hazel ignores it. "Who else is there?" she asks, as she writes down notes in a tattered notebook, based on her assessment of the bouncy ECG needles. "I don't know the super community that well yet. Have the Ravens done comparison research?"

I shake my head. "I doubt it. They wouldn't be interested in knowing about the other types of supers, just their own.

There's a good chance your research is the first of its kind in the world."

Hazel looks up, her expression arrested. "You think so? That's cool."

"And you'll be able to tell it all to a Mountain super so they can pass it down verbally to the other supers."

Hazel's horrified expression says it all. I let out a big belly laugh that gets me all the way to my toes.

32

Three days later, we still haven't heard from Seth. No messages. No texts. No answering my calls.

I'm sure he's fine.

Probably.

We're in the lab, I'm sitting in a padded chair, and Hazel is hooking me up to a whole bank of monitors. Her face is serious, and she's concentrating like she's taking her first-ever driving test.

I'm starting to feel like I'm half machine, I've got so many monitors attached to my body. "Are you sure all this is necessary?" I ask. "Surely there's a better way?"

"If you can only do this for me once, then I'm going to monitor every single little thing I can think of," says Hazel. Her eyes are focused on a screen next to me, the glowing light reflecting in her glasses.

"I guess." I'd rather be outside the house training with Zane and Blade, who seem to have forged some kind of forever-besties bond in the last couple of days.

I talked to my father back at the Earthbound compound and let him and the others know what happened and where we are. Hazel's research feels important enough that we decided to stay here a few more days. At least it feels like she might be able to explain what's happening to me a little more than anyone else has.

Maybe she'll figure out a way to slow it down, if she can't stop it. At this point, I'll take anything. She's also our best source of information on demons. If there's going to be a plague that we have to fight... well, I'd like to be on her side.

"Okay, I'm ready." Hazel steps back from the machines, like she's just been asked to set down her tools at some kind of competition.

Knowing Hazel, that's exactly what she was doing inside her head. "So what do you want me to do?" I ask.

"Try to use the spell web, just like you did the last time. We need to replicate one of your attacks. Just pull on the magic, and then let it go."

"And you know what to do if I have an attack?" I ask nervously.

"I'm great in a crisis," she says without one hint of irony or sarcasm.

I know, I was watching her closely for them. I hope she's serious. "What if this is the time it completely devours me?" I ask.

"It won't be. You'd have far more serious markers in your vitals. You're showing up as healthy and hearty. It'll be fine."

There's something about Hazel's confidence that's at once reassuring and contagious. And I've always been someone who prefers to do things rather than wait around. "Okay, here goes."

I sit up a little straighter in my chair, and the multitude of wires attached to my body follow my every movement. Closing my eyes, I find the glowing core of the spell web inside me. Its magic is pulsing, like it knows what we're doing and loves every minute of it.

I pull on the power of the spell web and wrap it around me. It feels warm and sheltering, like a winter coat that's actually part of me. I don't really understand why the spell web would hurt me. It always feels so protective. The attacks never feel familiar or personal. Maybe it's not true after all?

But maybe it is.

That could be the most insidious part of this whole situation. The very thing that makes me feel the safest in this world is the one thing that's going to kill me.

It's such a terrible thought, it makes me falter in my actions.

"What did you just do?" asks Hazel. "Something weird happened on the monitors."

"I hesitated."

"Interesting." Hazel writes a note on a pad next to the ECG. "Keep going. You can do this."

Taking a deep breath, I pull more of the spell web's magical covering into me. Because she's next to me, I know I'm using a little of Hazel's chalice powers. It feels unlike anything I've encountered so far—brisk and clean and golden. I feel Blade and Zane upstairs, and their magic is darker, more chaotic and brutal, almost harsh. I gather some of their magic to me as well. Then I search along the spell web to find other supernaturals who can spare a little magic for me to use.

As I search out past the house, I come across a clump of supers holding a weird pattern at the bottom of the cliff in front of Blade's property. They're in a boat in the water, too many for a casual fishing expedition. Maybe some kind of tourist operation? They're probably whale watchers, crowding the boat in search of the elusive mammals.

I take some of their magic too—not enough to make them anxious, but enough to help us with the testing. It's agitated and richly potent, but somehow bitter, like 90 percent chocolate. It fills me up, making me tremble with the power of all these different supers inside me. What can I do with all this magic? I've never just gathered power through the spell web for the sake of it before. My breathing is coming in gasps as I try to maintain control over everything I've just accumulated around me. It's wild and chaotic, whirling and twisting like it's excited about whatever I might be about to do.

I open my eyes, and everything inside the lab glows brighter than before. I can see all the details on the bench tops, the scrapes from some long ago accident, stains from experiments gone wrong. Looking closer, I can even see tiny particles moving inside the metal. It takes me a moment to realize I'm seeing the cells that make up the countertop. The details in the world around me are glorious, perfect—and overwhelming.

There's a noise beside me, and I turn. Hazel is speaking, I can see her mouth moving, but I can't differentiate the sounds she's making from the sound in the rest of the universe. It's coming at me all at once, like a symphony created by some master conductor. It's all working together, creating one enormous rush of noise so beautiful it makes my eyes well up.

The machines on the table next to me are part of the symphony, their needles scraping frantically up and down and their lights blinking furiously. Hazel is moving between the monitors, her expression fierce. It's like I'm watching everything that's happening from a distance, like some kind of weird puppet master, but unable to interact with anything I can see.

What am I supposed to do with the magic now? The idea was that I would gather it to me and then let it dissipate back out into the web. But the magic is curled around me, fizzing and buzzing, and there's no way to just let it go. It wants me to use it, to let it free into the world. That's what's supposed to happen when I gather the magic to me.

For a moment, the sensible, sane part of me—the bit that knows the plan and knows we're down in a basement lab with no place for the magic to actually go—tries to take control. But it loses out to the other part of me, the section of me that's wrapped in the glow of the spell web, unwilling to let such glorious magic go without using it for some sublime purpose.

My eyes wander the room, looking for a use, a problem, a solution to where to focus my magic. There's nothing much here, other than the machines—but they're all hooked up to me—and the countertops.

An image from an old movie pops into my head. *Beauty and the Beast*. Dancing furniture, people turned into housewares that twirl around an elegant house.

The lab's not exactly an elegant mansion, but it'll do. I lift one hand, and every single laboratory table in the room lifts itself off the floor. The room glows with the magic inside it, and the tables start twirling around the room, faster and faster, like whirling dervishes from a faraway land.

There's a screaming noise in my ear, and I struggle to break down the sound into one particle, one thing. I turn my head, and see Hazel right next to me, yelling at me, her eyes wide, her expression frightened.

Just as suddenly as it began, the dancing stops. The metal tables fall to the ground, back in the exact same rows they were in when they started. The magic is drained out of me, and I feel empty, like everything has been sucked from my body, and I'm just a bag of bones.

"Oh my God, Mei. I thought you were just going to let the magic go again," Hazel is saying next to me.

"I couldn't...." I manage weakly.

"Well, I got some great data from all of that. And it was kind of cool how you made the tables dance."

I nod wearily. The pain is coming, I can feel it worming its way into my body, the needles starting to prick my skin, and the fire ants wandering along my outer limbs, ready to begin the march to my central core. "It's coming," I say. "The attack."

Hazel turns back to me. "It hasn't happened already?" she asks anxiously. "That's not what all that was?" She gestures to the room.

We both look at the slightly disheveled lab, pieces of glass on the floor, notebooks strewn around.

On the far side of the room, there's a blue mist forming. I blink a couple of times, trying to figure out if I'm just imagining it. My eyes flick to Hazel to see if she's seeing what I'm seeing. She's watching it too.

"How annoying," she murmurs under her breath.

The glowing blue mist is expanding and quickly forming a tall, strange-looking demon in front of us. As it changes from a glowing blue monstrosity into a more solid demon, details begin to appear across its body. It's got gears and spokes and even a wheel sticking out of it. The demon seems to be half bike, half creature from another realm.

Even as the demon is growing and forming solidity, my body is deteriorating into a giant ball of agony. It feels like my imaginary fire ants have decided to have a party with some other equally evil creatures—I'm thinking scorpions and wasps—and they're all digging into my skin in every possible place. The pain is too much for me to bear, and I scream, a long torturous sound that echoes around the lab and comes back to me threefold as I squirm in the padded chair.

I can't stand up. I can't do anything about the enormous demon that's advancing on us. Hazel moves to stand in front of me, but she's shaking. This demon is twice the size of the one she killed for me at the prison.

She needs help. I try to stand, try to move, and find I can't. My body is too heavy, too filled with pain and torment. Instead of standing up, all I'm doing is fading into the background, my vision darkening.

Until there's nothing.

33

I wake to the sound of screaming.

Except it's not someone else, it's me.

There's a strong blue glowing light over everything, and I scream again. I can't move, I can't think, and screaming is the only thing I can think of to help. Maybe Zane or Blade will hear me.

The demon is clearly in control, or the blue glow wouldn't be over everything. I think of the darkness in its eyes, the lack of mercy or forgiveness.

The other demon, the one that chased me across the country, was angry at me for putting it in the bottle. Hazel was probably the person who put this one in a bottle too.

I struggle to move my arms, even my legs, but it's like my whole body has turned into a lead weight while I was unconscious. Rolling my head, I try to get it to an angle that allows me to see what terrible things the demon is doing to Hazel. The blue light is everywhere, coating the room like a blanket. I remember clearly what the other demon did to the old pawn shop owner, tearing him apart like he was nothing, flesh pulled from the bones.

I scream again, just with the frustration of not being able to move, or even to see. It's just like when I was turning into a dragon for the first time. Except this is worse because I know something awful is happening to Hazel.

My head rolls, and suddenly I can see her.

Except she's not being torn limb from limb. She's standing with her arms outstretched, blue light emanating from her body just like a demon. The demon is standing in front of her, its whole body in a stance of complete supplication. The unholy light in its eyes is gone, now it's looking at her like a puppy at its master.

How is she doing that?

I knew she could destroy the demons, but she's controlling this one like it's a child. An enormous, muscle-bound, frightening child willing to do her every command.

Hazel turns back to me, and her eyes are glowing blue, too. Her glasses are off, lying on the nearest bench top. Her brown hair is flying out in all directions, like there's some kind of unseen wind, and for a second I'm frightened. Maybe she's turned into a demon?

Maybe this isn't Hazel anymore?

This could be some new demon hybrid, who's about to kill me.

Hazel takes a step forward. I try to move; inside I'm struggling, forcing my arms and legs to do something more than just lie here. But I can't.

I scream again, but this time it's more of a snarl, a warning to whatever is inside Hazel.

And then suddenly, she's not blue anymore. It's Hazel, the researcher I've come to know. She grabs her glasses off the counter and puts them back on.

"Mei? Mei, are you okay?" she asks, as she walks back

over to me. She's peering into my face, trying to determine if I'm even awake.

I blink at her.

"You're awake. Thank goodness." She grabs something off a nearby shelf and brings a drink bottle with a silicone straw over to me. "Drink this. It'll help."

She puts the straw between my lips, and I suck the liquid up greedily. As soon as it touches my lips I realize it's not water. It's some kind of electrolyte drink, giving my body the energy it needs. Hazel was prepared for this situation, far more than I was.

How did she know?

I think she's just the kind of person who's prepared for anything. Prepared for the worst maybe?

Whatever it is, I'm grateful to the electrolytes that are now coursing through my body, sending little berry bursts of energy.

My fingers on my left hand manage a flicker of movement, and I grin. Give me a few minutes, and I'll be back to normal.

There's a crash from behind us, and Hazel turns around. The demon is moving around agitatedly, like it's trying to find a way out of the lab.

"I'm just going to finish dealing with this demon," says Hazel once I've finished the entire drink bottle. She turns back to the demon and raises her hands. She starts to glow again, and this time I'm watching with curiosity, not fear. She looks so confident, as if she knows exactly what she's doing.

Not bad for a woman who didn't even know what she was only a few months ago.

A gentle humming echoes around the room, and then a

song starts. I think it might be a David Bowie song, although I'm not sure.

The demon in front of her stops. Its eyes are wide, and its expression goes slack. It moves toward Hazel, its body blurring into mist the closer it gets. Once it's about a foot away, it stops, and it's just a glowing blue cloud, the particles whizzing around in front of Hazel. She lets out a single high-pitched note, and the mist enters Hazel's body through her stomach. She bunches herself up, rounding her back like a cat, and seems to focus on absorbing the demon.

Abruptly all sound in the lab stops, and Hazel stands up normally.

She clears her throat and turns back to me. "Well, that's taken care of. Now to look at your results."

I've got enough control to nod. I want to know what all her machines tell her about me, about what's happening inside me. But first....

"Have you...?" I clear my throat, not sure why I'm stumbling over the question. "Did you...?"

"Attached myself to these sensors while I deal with a demon?" asks Hazel, with her eyebrows raised.

I nod.

"Not yet. It's a complicated process. And I think my singing might actually break a couple of them if I was attached, and close enough."

"You should do it," I say.

"It was pretty amazing to see what happened while you were using your magic," she says, not quite answering. "I've never seen anything like it."

My heart jumps. "What did you learn?"

Hazel shakes her head. "I'll need to look over the data properly before I know anything definitely. It's too early." She starts removing the sensors covering my body.

"I don't have a huge amount of time," I say, a frown creasing my forehead.

Hazel pauses and looks at me. "How do you know?"

"Carrick's grandfather—"

"The one who had it handed down verbally?" says Hazel, her voice scornful.

"The attacks are getting worse."

"That's more useful information."

"So you think he might be wrong? That I might not be going to implode?"

Hazel glances at the sensors and then back at me. "I think it's likely that the spell web is too powerful for one supernatural to carry around inside them. The fact that it's devouring you one piece at a time also seems highly possible. We just don't know how fast that might be happening."

"It could be years, not days?" I ask hopefully.

Hazel nods absently, her focus on looking over the output on the sensors. "Of course, it could also be hours, not days."

"What? How can—"

An alarm, high-pitched and piercing, starts up all around us.

"What the hell?" I say, pulling off the last of the sensors from my arm.

34

We rush out of the lab and up the stairs to the main floor. Zane and Blade are coming down the hall toward us.

"It's the perimeter alert," says Blade grimly.

"Who is it?" I ask.

He shakes his head. "I don't know. I'm guessing it's the SIG, but I don't have confirmation. They don't have any markings."

Zane glances over at me. "It could be any one of Mei's enemies. She seems to collect them like baseball cards."

"Hey. You're not exactly Mr. Personality either. You just haven't had enough time awake to make enemies."

He laughs, and I see the same anticipation in his eyes that I feel. The thrill of pitting ourselves against someone, of fighting.

"There's a back way out," says Blade. His voice is reluctant, but he's looking at Hazel.

"How many?" I ask, not willing to give up on a fight. Just sitting here is driving me nuts. I'm already back to almost full strength after my attack.

"Twelve, maybe as many as fifteen. They're coming up the cliff face."

I remember the supers I took power from while I was gathering the strength of the spell web to me. "They were in a boat. Down below." I clench my fists. Why didn't I figure it out immediately? "When we were testing the spell web, I felt them. I thought they were some kind of tourist boat."

"With guns?" asks Zane drily.

I glare at him. "We can take them, between the two of us. Blade can go with Hazel, protect her. It's probably my fault they're here."

Blade shakes his head. "I promised your father I'd look after you. You need to come with us. We can leave Zane to distract them for a while. He's strong, he can take care of them."

Zane gives another snort of laughter. "If you think I can take care of myself, you should see Mei. I'm nothing on her."

Blade frowns over at me, looking me up and down. He clearly doesn't believe Zane.

"Look, I'm going out there," I say impatiently. "The more time we waste arguing, the harder it will be. But you can't stop me."

Blade looks at Zane, who shrugs. "Don't look at me, Blade. She's her own person, makes her own decisions."

"Dad would expect me to go out there," I say. "His idea of protection was to let me be raised by an S.I.G. agent and a protector who taught me how to fight."

"I'm staying with Hazel. She's too important," says Blade. He lifts his watch. "I have all the cameras set to my watch. If you run into any problems, I'll come help."

I nod and then gesture with my head at Zane. "Let's go." I stalk down the corridor, halting at the door to the living room. I glance back, and Zane is right behind me. He grins. I open the door slowly, peering through. It's still light outside, although it's late afternoon, and the sun is casting long shadows across the room.

"Did you see where they were coming up?"

"Blade showed me the camera images. Up the side of the cliff, over there." Zane points to the far side of the property, where there's some cover of trees and bushes.

"They planned this out. Knew where to come up," I say softly.

"Seems that way."

"How long ago was that? Could they have they made it up?"

"Only one way to find out," says Zane.

I step into the living room area, keeping myself low. We run across the room to the glass doors, and I open them, still watching carefully, trying to find the intruders. I send a pulse out over the spell web, searching.

There they are. Seven supers on the cliff top, and another five still climbing. "Over there," I say, pointing. "Some have made it to the top. They're spreading out, making a perimeter."

"How are we going to do this?" asks Zane. "In dragon form?"

I hesitate. I really want a fight, hand to hand. "You change, I'm going to stay in human form for now. You take out the ones on the cliff face first. Burn them up. I'll approach the ones who've made it up. We'll meet in the middle."

"Take care, okay?" says Zane.

"Yeah, you too."

I open the sliding door and step out onto the tiled deck, followed closely by Zane. He's dropping his clothes as he goes, and moments later I feel the pull on the spell web as he transforms into an enormous black and golden dragon.

I glance back, unable to help myself from basking in the glory of another dragon. Enormous wings spread out wide, his dark scales reflecting the setting sun, and his black eyes glittering with menace. Perfect. That'll teach whoever's attacking without provocation.

Even with provocation.

I use the distraction provided by Zane to crouch low and run along the side of the property, down through the same trees they're using as cover. There are some panicked shouts from the men who have spread out down the cliff line. They're concentrating on the enormous dragon that's just appeared instead of the small woman running toward them.

Too bad.

The first man is so focused on Zane, he doesn't even see me as I run at him from the side, punching him twice in the kidney before slamming an upper cut punch squarely into the middle of his chin. He slides to the ground, unconscious.

The next man sees me but doesn't have time to pull his gun into position before I slam into him. His gun goes flying, and we skid along in the dirt, arms wrapped around each other. If I weren't a dragon and in charge of the spell web, this would have been a bad idea. He's much bigger than me, and he should be the stronger by a country mile. As it is, he grabs me around the waist, clearly believing he's about the take charge.

I simply windmill out my arms, breaking his grip, and bring my knee up into his groin. He grunts, but to his credit doesn't move away. I bring up my elbow for a roundhouse into his cheek, and then roll off him, coming up into a crouch. He's fractionally slower than I am, and his eyes are narrowed on me.

It's the weirdest thing. It's like he doesn't realize I'm a dragon. Like he hasn't been properly briefed over who he might find here.

What's their mission? Who's he fighting for?

Problem is, I don't have time to interrogate him right now, I have another five men to disable up on the cliff top. I take a running leap at him, twisting in midair and flicking my leg into a high kick that hits him squarely in the chest. He grunts as he moves back, bringing up his guard. I don't give him too much time to think, moving in for the final knock out. Three punches later and he's on the ground, unmoving.

I move onto the next man, who's positioned with his back to me, watching Zane swoop down on the men still climbing the cliff face. I can see he's debating whether to go help or stay in the relative safety of his current position. They've made it easy for me by spacing themselves out like this.

I keep moving forward, my whole focus on bringing the next man down. Even if nothing else in the world is going right, I can still do this.

I can still fight.

He has a longer reach than me, but I'm faster and stronger, and if I'm honest, far sneakier. Si's voice is in my head, telling me not to rely on the spell web, so I don't pull extra power from it like I could. I don't really want to risk it knocking me out before my job here is done anyway.

Turns out, he's easy to knock unconscious; he's too distracted by Zane.

There are four more men up the top of the cliff. Two are helping the men still on the cliff face, standing at the top, holding the ropes steady. At least they're not deserting their fellow incursion teammates.

I'm almost on them when something slams into me from the side, and I'm sent skidding along the top of the cliff with something large and dressed in black attached to me. In fact, it's dry, smooth rock, and we get perilously close to the edge before our momentum slows. I slam both my fists into his ears, and when he lets go, I elbow him in the face. He howls like a baby and holds his hands up to his bleeding nose.

I roll off him again and stand up, panting from the unexpectedness of the attack. I turn to see what's happened to the other men, but I've underestimated my current opponent's ability to ignore the pain, and he slams into me again. This time he's got just enough momentum that we both fly through the air and off the side of the cliff.

And then we're hurtling down toward the ocean as it batters the rocks below.

35

The man lets go of me, clearly attempting to save himself by maneuvering out over the water. Without even thinking about it, I transform. Sparks of pain race quickly through my body, and then it's the glory of flight as my enormous wings snap out and take me upward on the next available current.

The man who pushed us over falls to the sea, screaming as he goes.

I twitch my wings to one side and swing round, back to the last three men still standing on the cliff top. They've pulled out their weapons, some kind of weird gun that I don't recognize. They're aiming in my direction, and I have a moment of fear, wondering if this is some new weapon the Earthbound left behind and never had a chance to use.

They shoot, and I dive, unwilling to test the weapons, just in case. I'm too slow, and a sting of pain hits my flank. Looking down I see a slight raise where one of the bullets has hit me and bounced off my dragon skin. They're a little more forceful than usual, but my body still has a natural protection.

I roar, fire burning up inside my belly. These soldiers aren't here to mess around. They've got guns designed to kill whoever they're meant for. I send a blazing line of fire down toward the last two men and burn them into a crisp.

Zane swoops past, sending a rush of air at me. *What took you so long?* he asks smugly.

I had seven, you only had five, I say peevishly.

Zane lets out a huffing dragon laugh. *Excuses, excuses.*

We swoop through the air for a few more minutes, both of us enjoying being in our dragon bodies. I switch to heat sensing, making sure that we haven't left any of the attackers.

I'm going to put the ones I knocked out down on their boat again.

You didn't kill them all?

I give Zane a look and then swoop down, grabbing an unconscious man and dumping him into the boat. I grab the next one and do that same. But the third man, I take back to the entrance of Blade's house, and dump him by the door. I want to know who they were after, what their mission was.

Zane comes in behind me and lands, transforming and getting dressed. "You want to interrogate him?" he asks.

I nod.

"I'll be scarier for him if you stay in dragon form."

I nod again.

Zane crouches down and shakes the man gently. "Wakey, wakey." I move into position on the other side of the soldier.

The soldier groans, lifting his hands to his head where I punched him.

It's easy to tell the moment he remembers where he is and what he was doing. He stiffens, and his eyes flick open. He sees Zane and jerks away from him. Then he sees me.

His eyes widen, and he scrambles back, away from me, toward Zane again. It doesn't do him any good. I simply move my neck down, and my enormous head is right in front of him again. I snarl, giving him a good look at my teeth.

"If you don't want her to tear you apart, you have a few questions to answer for us," says Zane.

The man shakes his head, but he's looking at me with wide, terrified eyes. I let a little smoke tease its way out of my mouth, my hot breath pushing down over the man's face.

"Have you ever barbecued food? That's kind of what it's like to feel the fire from a dragon's belly," says Zane, and his voice is almost conversational.

Our prisoner makes a strangled sound and tries frantically to move away from me again. I lift one paw and lean down, pinning his shirt to the ground with my claw. There's fire forming inside my stomach, and I let a few of the flames rumble up my throat. The sound is like thunder forming on the horizon, and his eyes dart between me and Zane.

"Can you control it?" he asks Zane, his voice squeaking. "If I tell you, it won't burn me alive anyway?"

"*She* has a mind of her own," says Zane. "But if you promise to tell us what you know, I'm sure she'll probably let you live."

I lean in again and show him my teeth. He struggles to move away.

"Probably," repeats Zane.

Our prisoner looks between us, clearly torn. "Okay."

"What's your mission?"

"To get the girl. The one who can see demons."

"Why?"

"Our boss wants her. Thinks she's important to his plans."

"Who's your boss?"

The man hesitates. "I can't say."

Flames flicker at the edges of my lips. I let the prisoner feel the heat from them.

"Okay, okay! His name is Connor McKenzie."

The guy who's helping the director. I glance at Zane and he's looking back at me with the same recognition in his face.

"What does he think Hazel can do for him?"

"He wants to control the demons. Use them for charging up the power grid for humans and supers. His dream is cheap, easy power that everyone can use."

Somehow I doubt that. More likely it's accessible power for the masses that makes him loads of money if he's anything like the guy that Hazel has described to us.

"What's with the new guns?" asks Zane. He rubs his side absently as he asks the question. Clearly he was hit as well.

"One of Connor's researchers developed them. Supposed to give us an edge against other supers."

I growl, starting to really dislike this Connor guy.

"What about Blade?"

"We were supposed to get rid of him if we could. It wasn't the primary mission, but it was a goal. It was supposed to be an easy mission. There were only supposed to be two of them here. The boss was confident."

"Where were you going to take her?"

The man hesitates. I growl. He cringes back. "I don't know! It wasn't part of my mission protocol."

"Who knew?"

"Ralph."

"The guy on the boat?" asks Zane.

He nods.

There was no guy on the boat when I dumped the two unconscious men into it. I'm assuming Ralph is dead.

"How long have you worked for Connor?"

"A couple of years."

"What's he like?"

"He doesn't fraternize with us much. He's a busy guy. Just tells Ralph what he wants us to do, and we do it."

"Have you met him? What does he look like?"

"He's tall, good-looking. A super amazing guy. Too good to hang out with the likes of us." The guy's eyes take on a hazy edge, and I notice a few extra threads of the spell web hanging around his body for the first time. Like someone has used it to give him a little something extra.

Didn't Hazel say Connor was half Siren?

It must be how he gathers loyalty, using his siren abilities, no matter how weak.

I sit back on my haunches. We've got enough information from this guy. I look at Zane, and he shrugs up at me.

"I'm done," he says. "You can sort him out."

The prisoner squeaks and tries to scramble away, even though there's nowhere else to go. "You promised. You said she wouldn't barbecue me!"

"I didn't say she wouldn't eat you," says Zane mildly.

I pick the struggling soldier up and leap into the air. He screams, wriggling his legs like he thinks that will save him. Swooping down over the water, I soar close to the boat, and drop him inside, just high enough that his fall will hurt.

Those bullets they were shooting weren't supposed to stun.

They were supposed to *kill supers*. Including Blade.

36

"He definitely said it was Connor?" asks Hazel for the third time.

We're all back in the living room. I'm now wearing some of Hazel's clothes, seeing as I destroyed my last set.

"He did. He was acting like he'd had a bit of fairy juice to keep him going," says Zane, his face screwed up with distaste.

"That's Connor's specialty," says Hazel, her expression pinched. "He was coming for me. And he knew about this place, Blade." She looks up at Blade.

He nods. "It's been compromised. We're not staying here. Pack your things." He looks to us. "Will you take us to another of my safe houses?"

"Of course," I say. I try to leave it at that, but I can't stop myself from asking, "How many do you have?"

"Five."

"All like this?" I gaze innocently around at the fancy furnishings.

Blade gives me a look. "No. They're all different. This

was my favorite." He glances at Hazel. "And it has the best lab."

It's not the only lab, I note. *Just the best one.* This dude is completely smitten with Hazel.

Zane clears his throat. "Getting out of here's a good idea. We need to do it ASAP. We don't know what else that Connor dude might have planned, and this place is exposed. If he decides that no one can have Hazel if he can't have her...."

I nod and push myself into standing position. "Do we need to take anything from your lab?" I ask Hazel. I don't want her to lose any of the information about my attacks.

She shakes her head. "It's all connected wirelessly. All the information that the machines gave me is in the cloud."

"Take everything," warns Blade. "We need to assume that we won't be coming back here."

"The only thing I want is my notebook," says Hazel.

"We only have the clothes on our backs," I say, looking over at Zane who nods in agreement. "The ones I'm wearing aren't even mine." I glance down at the jeans and T-shirt of Hazel's that I put on. Ripped jeans. *Stranger Things* T-shirt.

Hazel grins and nods before disappearing down the hall toward the lab.

"We need to—" Blade's phone rings, and he pulls it from his back pocket, frowning down at the screen. "Your father is calling me," he says, glancing up at me.

"Is that unusual?"

"It's a burner phone that no one should know the number for," says Blade.

"Answer it," I say, trying to stay calm. "And don't worry, he's an enigma to everyone."

"Hello, Damien," says Blade sternly, like he's talking to a naughty kid.

I can hear Dad's voice on the other end. He sounds as calm as ever, but something is up. Is Dad okay? Has the director attacked the Earthbound compound again? I wouldn't put it past him.

"Okay, sure. I'll tell them. Yes. We'll come too. Okay. Fine." Blade's voice is sounding tighter and tighter. His face is grim.

I can't stop the fear that's crawling along my body. What's happened?

Blade hangs up and turns to me. "Seth's been trying to get in touch with you for the last hour."

I blink. "My phone was in my pocket when I changed in midair. It's somewhere in the ocean by now."

"There's a problem. Demons are swarming Newport News. Hundreds of them. Your father says Seth and the Ravens need our help. Your father is already on his way, along with a few of the others from the compound."

"Is Seth okay?" I ask, my heart racing.

"For now. But there are too many demons. We have to help them." He glances in the direction Hazel disappeared. "All of us."

"We need to prepare for a long flight. Grab first aid kits, blankets, and food," I say. "We'll have to sleep rough tonight."

Blade nods, and strides into the hallway. "You get whatever you think we'll need from the cupboard and fridge, pack it in this bag," he says, grabbing a military style backpack from a cabinet in the hallway and handing it to me.

"You'll get everything else?"

"Yes. We'll meet back in the yard in ten." He disappears down the hall without another word.

Zane and I search the kitchen, grabbing drinks, and any packaged food that will travel easily. We end up with granola bars, chocolate, beef jerky, Fruit Roll-Ups, and cashew nuts.

"Breakfast of champions," I say drily.

"It's only to give us energy so we can keep going," says Zane. "Speed seems like it's of the essence."

Concern for Seth squeezes at my heart, and I look away, adding another water bottle to the bag.

"Hey, he's gonna be fine," says Zane, his voice softening. "He's got two dragons on his side. And he's a freaking phoenix for crying out loud."

I nod. "He can take care of himself. I know he can. It's just...."

"I know. Let's get out of here. Get on the road."

Zane and I race into the backyard and change, leaving the bags with our clothes and the supplies on the lawn. Blade and Hazel appear soon after, both looking grim but determined. Part of me is worried about Hazel. She's hasn't been trained to fight like the rest of us. But then I remember her and the demon in the lab.

She's far more powerful than she looks at first glance.

They both put on a bag, and Hazel climbs on my back, while Blade gets up on Zane. He looks much more comfortable on Zane's back than last time, which makes me wonder if he's been training on dragon-back while we were down in the lab testing things out.

We leap into the air, and I try not to worry that we won't get there in time. It's a long flight from the west coast to the east coast. Even going as fast as we can, it'll probably take us a good ten to twelve hours nonstop, at least. And I don't think Hazel or Blade will last for that long on dragon-back without a break. So we're not going to get to Seth until tomorrow.

And something is telling me that it might be too long.

everal hours later, we land at a twist in the Missouri River, somewhere in South Dakota. It's dark, sometime around midnight, I'm guessing.

Hazel stumbles to the ground and sits down straight away. "We need to invent some kind of seat. Something to make riding dragon-back at least a little more comfortable," she says wearily, leaning back against my flank.

Not a bad idea. Although I'd only let certain people use it. I blink down at her, trying to make sure she's okay. She's a little pale, her face glowing by the moonlight, but otherwise her only problem seems to be exhaustion.

I'll stay in dragon form, I say to Zane. *Keep watch. I'm too agitated to sleep.*

You go first watch. Wake me in two hours, says Zane firmly. *We all need rest.*

Zane changes into human form and puts on his clothes. There's a stand of trees next to the river, and they all get comfortable under the canopy, using the blankets Blade packed to sit on. Blade pulls out some of the rations from the bag, and they all drink and grab a snack, trying to revive after that long streak in the air. I'm not hungry. There's no way I can even think about eating right now. Seth's face is running through my mind. I only just got him back; the thought of losing him again is too much.

"Remember, Mei. Wake me in two hours," says Zane. "I mean it."

I nod absently, but I plan to give him more than just a couple of hours. There's really no point me attempting to sleep right now. I'm too hyped up.

They settle themselves down under the blankets while I get comfortable next to the tree, tucking my body into position like a giant cat, giving them some protection from the elements. It's not long before they're all asleep, and I'm left alone with my thoughts.

I gaze out into the night sky, letting the sounds of the insects and animals flow over me like a gentle lullaby. I spend the next three hours listening to the water gurgling over rocks, weaving past reeds, and gushing through the shallows. I curl the spell web around me like a blanket, weaving its strength into mine. If there's a way for me to consistently defeat demons, it has to be through the spell web. There has to be some kind of balance between using it and not using it so much that it knocks me out and makes me useless.

But I don't think there is. My only real option seems to be to use my dragon powers and to leave the spell web out of it. I can't afford to be unconscious just when the others need me. And this isn't one demon. This is a demon plague. Hundreds of demons, Blade said.

Jeff's voice in my head is the only thing that consoles me about this situation. *You don't need to use your other powers, Mei. You have the ability to overcome any opponent. Just use what we've taught you.*

What I don't understand is why Newport News? What's there that's causing the demon plague? Is this a personal attack? Someone trying to get at Seth and the Ravens? Is it something to do with Connor McKenzie? Or is this about the director? He seems to have more involvement in the demon plague than we realized. Perhaps instead of trying to clean it up, he's part of the formation of it? If he's in with Connor, that seems possible.

These thoughts swirl around in my head as I watch out over the landscape. The others sleep restlessly, none of them completely settled.

About three hours after we stopped, I wake Zane. He blearily wakes up, his eyes red, his body slow. I regret waking him right away. He must have needed it more than I realized.

"You need to transform and sleep, Mei," he says. "It's not good to stay in dragon form for too long. Think of Sergei." Zane's been helping the Russian dragon with his mood swings and bursts of anger, but it's not easy. Sergei is still not entirely stable.

It's the only argument that's guaranteed to get me to change, so I do as he says, grabbing my clothes and settling down under the blanket that Zane just vacated.

I close my eyes and surprisingly fall asleep. My sleep is filled with dreams of Seth being chased by glowing balls of light. When someone shakes me awake, I jerk up, holding my arm in a block, and whack Zane on the shoulder. He's in human form.

"Sorry," I say. "Bad dreams."

"No problem," he says, ruefully rubbing his arm. "But it's time to get up. We need to eat and get on our way."

The sky is lightening all around us, but the sun hasn't quite managed to rise just yet. It's still early. Blade and Hazel are rummaging around in the food bags and pulling out our options.

"Hmmm. Chocolate for breakfast," says Hazel. "Strangely not as appealing as I would have expected." She pulls out a granola bar instead and settles back onto one of the blankets.

I pull out a couple bits of jerky and sit down on a tree root. "So what exactly did Dad say? What's the plan?"

"All he said was that they were already on their way to Newport."

"How?"

"Dragon-back."

I frown. The only other dragons are Sergei and Elena. Both of them seem like less than perfect choices. Carrick doesn't trust Elena, and Sergei... well, no one trusts him to do what he's supposed to do.

"When were they expecting to get there? Where do we meet?"

"He said to call when we got close. He'd let us know where he was."

I clench my teeth together, trying to hold down the frustration. What if something happens to them before we get there? What if we call, and no one answers? But none of that is Blade's fault. And there's no point taking it out on him.

"So what are our plans? What can we do against a demon plague?" I ask. A little sarcastically.

Hazel chooses to ignore my sarcasm. "I can take care of a few demons at a time, but according to Blade, there are hundreds of them. I brought some bottles with me, and a few other smaller devices. They'll suck individual demons inside them."

"What will kill them?" I ask.

"Blade has a special knife that does them in," says Hazel.

"Unless he has a second one, that's also not helpful."

"High-pitched sound messes with them. Really high has the potential to kill them, although I've never tested that theory."

"So we just have to scream?"

"Well, I know that my scream kills them. But that's kinda my thing," says Hazel, her expression concerned. "I don't know if your scream is going to be high-pitched enough."

"What else?"

"They're beings of pure energy. They're hard to kill."

"Sounds like the perfect energy grid," I say grimly. "Maybe you're wrong? Maybe Connor has a better solution than you realize? Maybe he's just collecting them together so he can capture them and put them into some kind of energy machine that just happens to be located at Newport News."

"I never took you for the type to listen to fairy tales," says Hazel, her eyes serious.

38

I don't feel any better informed on how I'm going to fight demons when we stop just outside Newport News and Blade phones my father. Zane and I transform back into human form and stretch our legs as Blade dials the number my father gave him.

There's no answer for a long time, and I'm about to give up on Dad, and assume he's been devoured by glowing blue demons, when the call is connected.

"Hello? Damien?" says Blade.

I hear a voice on the other end, but it's not Dad. I don't know why I know; I just do.

"Yes. Damien called us, asked us to come and help. No. Yes, that's right." Blade's voice is carefully neutral, like he doesn't want to let on his real feelings to whoever he's talking to. "I'm sorry, I can't tell you that. No. I don't know you. I won't—"

Blade looks up. "He hung up."

"Who was it?"

"Some guy named Evan. Seemed pretty hostile."

"Seth's father. Where's my Dad?"

"He wouldn't tell me."

"Is he okay?"

"Didn't say."

"What *did* he say?" I say in exasperation.

"He wanted to know where we were. Said he'd send someone to get us."

"You didn't—?"

"No."

"So what now?" asks Zane.

"I've been here before," I say. "I can get us to Seth's brother's place. He might be a pain in the ass, but I'm sure he's on our side. He wouldn't double-cross Seth. Not a second time."

"You hope," growls Zane.

"What other choice do we have?" I snap. "We don't know where any of the others are. We don't know where the demons are—"

"I could probably help with that," says Hazel cautiously.

"It would be good to know where they are, but we can't go racing in on our own. We need a plan, a concerted effort with all the people who are part of this."

Blade nods in agreement. "If there are hundreds of them, we need to check in with the others, find out how best to destroy them."

"Let's go to Seth's brother first, and figure it out from there."

It doesn't take us long to make the flight from the outskirts of town to the suburban house. We land in the backyard, and this time no one comes to greet us on the steps. I transform, dress, and then storm into the house. It's unlocked. I stride about inside, ready to yell at whoever I find. But it's disconcertingly empty.

I'm about to declare it empty when I remember how

Seth and I left here the first time. I race to the hall closet under the stairs, pushing aside the coats and sports paraphernalia. I find the latch and push open the door into the hidden hallway, grab the flashlight and keys from the little shelf, and run down the corridor. I can hear Blade following behind me.

"Mei, slow down. You don't know what you're running into," he calls out in a loud whisper.

The words slow me down. He's right. I'm rushing because I'm afraid, but it's making me not think properly. I try to remember what happened last time, where we went. At the end of the corridor, there's a familiar door. I hesitate and wait until Blade catches up with me.

"The others are waiting in the house. Just in case," says Blade.

I nod, shoving the key into the lock. I turn it quickly and push open the door.

The garage is empty. The cars that filled it last time are no longer here. What does that mean? Have they all fled? Where have they gone?

I walk into the space, turning around and around, trying to find some clue, something they've left behind.

Why did they run? Do they have some information that we don't? Is the demon plague really so bad? I don't know the answers, and they're gnawing at me like rats on a bone.

I'm about to head back to the door when a slight noise from the far end of the garage makes me still. It sounded like a cough. I glance over at Blade, and his whole being is focused on the same darkened corner of the room. There are some big metal cabinets, next to an old wooden workbench covered in tools and spare car parts.

I motion to Blade, and we both move silently toward the cabinets. There's no other sound, and I might've thought I imagined it if Blade hadn't heard the same thing. I move to stand to one side of the metal cabinet. Just in case someone decides to start shooting, I open the catch from the side, not willing to give them an easy target.

The doors swing open, screeching on metal hinges that don't get used often. I peer around the door, and find Tracey and two of her kids looking back up at me. Tracey's usually composed face has mascara leaking down where she's been crying, and the kids look disheveled. Tracey blinks her sharp Eagle eyes at me.

"What the hell?" I say, unable to be more coherent.

"Oh thank God, Mei. It's terrible. The Ravens, they've gone mental. They took Seth and Mike. Your father let them. The only reason they didn't get us too is that Mike made me hide here with the kids. We can never be sure what the Ravens will do to the kids. They have such ideas in their heads." The words are tumbling out like she's been holding them in tight for too long, and tears start streaming down her blotchy face again as she clutches the two kids.

"Where are the other kids?" I ask. I vaguely remember more of them.

"In the other cabinet."

I open the doors, and two boys burst out, ready to hit me with wrenches.

"It's okay, it's okay! I'm here to help," I yell, fending off their advances.

"Benny, Charlie, stop it. That's your Aunty Mei." Tracey's climbing out of her hiding place, and the boys rush to her, their faces crumpling from the effort of holding themselves strong in the face of their obvious fear. She holds all her kids tight to her body, her eyes scrunched closed.

"Shall we go back to the main house?" I ask.

Tracey shakes her head. "They'll be watching there. We can't go out there again."

I glance at Blade and he nods. "I'll go fetch the other two." He takes off at a run, clearly not liking to leave Hazel alone for too long. Like he doesn't think Zane would be able to protect her properly. It's hard not to grin after him.

"There are more of you? Did you come in quietly?" asks Tracey anxiously.

I raise my eyebrows. "As quietly as a dragon can ever come in. It's early morning, not many people around."

Tracey's face falls. "They'll come looking for you if you don't leave soon. You have to go back out, and leave, then come back later, at night."

"We can stay for a while longer. They'll expect us to regroup, right?"

Tracey nods uncertainly.

"I need you to tell me exactly what's happened. And where the Ravens have taken Mike and Seth."

"Evan's gone off the deep end. He's always been a little... intense. He never approved of me, even if he seemed to like me most of the time. But since Seth turned phoenix, he's been unbearable. He sees it as his chance to get back in with the Raven hierarchy." She makes a face. "Marrying me put Mike, and by association Evan, in the black books with many in the community."

"I'm guessing Seth wasn't playing nice?"

Tracey shook her head, a wry grin on her face. "He never did play well with others. And he's basically resisting every effort of his father to bring him back into the fold. When Evan brought that girl over—" Tracey breaks off and looks at me warily.

"He told me about the marrying thing," I say, trying to

keep the jealousy out of my voice. I know I can trust Seth, he would never do anything to hurt me.

"Well, Seth told him to go jump. Evan didn't like that. He told us that the demons were gathering and that the only way to save us all was to marry Seth off to a powerful Raven girl—who just happens to be the daughter of the current Head Augury."

She sees my puzzled look.

"The Ravens have a council of Auguries, who are entrusted with determining the future based on their observations," she explains.

Just then, Blade, Hazel and Zane come through the door, and they all nod at Tracey.

"This is Hazel and Zane," I say. "Blade is the surly guy you met before."

"Hi there," says Tracey, her sharp eyes moving over the other three, as if committing their faces to memory.

I can't help but wonder what she's thinking. I clear my throat, trying not to let my curiosity overcome my focus. "So the power of a phoenix would be enough to lift up the Augury in the Raven Community?"

"Absolutely."

It's soothing to hear the political machinations around Seth's supposed marriage. It's more about the politics than the magic after all.

"But Evan got into a rage and disappeared. When he came back, he came with reinforcements, and they took Mike and Seth. He doesn't like it when he doesn't get his way."

"So as well as an influx of demons, we've got to deal with a kidnapping?" asks Blade sharply.

"When it rains it pours," I say drily.

"Does that mean we can't expect any help from the Ravens?" Blade is looking at Tracey with narrowed eyes.

"I don't know about the rest of them. Evan is the only Raven that I see on a regular basis other than Mike. We're basically banned from the community."

"I'm sorry. I didn't know it was as bad as that," I say.

Tracey makes a face. "To be fair, I don't mind it. They can be a bit much sometimes. It's Mike who feels the loss. He used to be close to his father growing up. Now Evan can't look at him without feeling resentful."

"Because he thought Mike was going to be a phoenix?"

"He spent all that time with Mike, when he should have been spending a bit more time with his other son, the one he thought was too small and weak to be useful." Tracey's tone is condemning of Evan.

"You don't like him?"

"It's not a matter of dislike. I just don't like the way he's treating Mike, especially since Seth turned."

"What's he been doing?" I've always had a problem with Evan but I didn't realize he'd started being an asshole to Mike and Tracey as well.

"Just ignoring him. And he's started being mean to the kids. He always used to at least give them the time of day." She hugs the youngest child closer to her.

"Do you know where they would have taken them?"

"Maybe the headquarters for the raven clan's business in these parts? It's downtown. They often congregate there for meetings."

"Then that's where we have to go."

39

We leave Tracey and the kids where they are, although Tracey doesn't get back into the cabinets. I grab her a blanket and give her some of our food (mostly the chocolate for the kids) so they can have a picnic.

And then we leave to go to the Augury's headquarters.

"You think this is a good idea?" asks Blade as we go back outside.

"The other option is to just hang out here until they decide to come in and try to force us to go somewhere. They took Mike and Seth without too much trouble."

Zane growls. "They wouldn't take two dragons, a chalice, and a jaguar so easily."

"It might have been that Seth and Mike decided to go with them to keep them away from the kids," I say soothingly.

"Where do you think your father is?"

I shake my head, and my gut starts to hurt. "I don't know." This situation is turning into a complete mess.

"Everything seems to lead back to the Ravens," says

Hazel. "Sometimes the simplest answer is the correct one, even after testing."

"She's right. Which means we go find the Ravens," I say.

We transform, and Hazel shoves our clothes in her bag before climbing back on me.

"We really need to do something about a harness, or something," she mutters to herself.

I'm not a horse, I think at her, but she can't hear.

You're starting to get a bit of a horsey nose, says Zane, laughter in his voice.

I let out a huff of breath and take off.

We fly into the sky and head south toward the industrial areas by the water. Tracey said the Augury's business was called Raven Technologies, and she gave us an address in the industrial area near the port. When we get closer, we can see a group of large white buildings just next to the highway, and within sight of the water.

This is it, I say to Zane. He nods, and we soar down, landing in a grassy patch behind a building and across the road from the headquarters, so we can change.

"Do you think they'll be expecting us?" asks Hazel anxiously as we crouch behind the building we're using as cover and check out Raven Technologies.

"It's possible. Tracey thought they were watching the house." I glance up into the sky, searching for a Raven. "They might even have followed us. I guess that's a benefit of being a Raven, it's easier to hide in the sky than when you're a dragon."

"Not many other benefits, I would have thought," says Zane grimly. His eyes are blazing, and he's practically radiating heat. He's primed and ready to storm the Raven Headquarters.

"What do they do here?" asks Hazel, staring up at the enormous buildings in front of us.

"It's an aviation company," I say. "Mostly helicopters, Tracey said." Kinda appropriate.

"What's the best way in?" asks Zane.

I narrow my eyes at the building. "I'm tempted by the idea of just going up to the front door and knocking. But I think perhaps we should make a bit more of an entrance."

"And how will we do that, exactly?" asks Blade.

"I was thinking dragons?"

"You won't get a dragon through any of those doors," says Zane.

He's right. "So we get inside, and then change."

"Which works only if they aren't expecting us," says Blade, searching the skies above us. "And if their security system is far less impressive than the name Raven Technologies implies."

"Maybe they won't expect us to be so bold?"

"This all seems risky," Blade's expression is conflicted.

"I don't think we should wait around. We have to storm this place, and we have to do it now, before they can get themselves too organized." I glance at Hazel. "Maybe Hazel and Blade should wait outside while Zane and I check this place out."

Blade nods his head in complete agreement, but Hazel frowns. "You need someone to carry the supplies and to be your backup. Who's going to speak to the Ravens when you're in dragon form?" She glares at Blade. "And I refuse to stay out here by myself, just in case you're about to suggest that."

I nod sharply. "Okay, we're all in this together, then. Keep an eye out for each other, don't let anyone take us by surprise. Our aim is to get Mike and Seth out of there as fast as possible, and to reconvene somewhere else to figure out where my dad and the others are, before we take on the demons."

Everyone nods. I lead the way down the footpath, trying to pretend that we're just an ordinary group of people walking down the street. We cross the road, and my heart starts to beat faster. We really have no idea what we're going to find inside these buildings. It could be hundreds of Ravens, armed to the teeth. They could have weapons from the Earthbound—they always seem to turn up at really inconvenient times—or some other weapons that I haven't even come across yet.

There's no sign from the outside of the building about what to expect. We walk past once, just to check out the doors and assess security cameras and guards, but there's nothing obvious.

"Either they're really good, or they don't care about security," says Blade out the side of his mouth.

"We have to assume they're really good," I say. I point to a door on the side of the building, near the front. "We go in through that entry. I can pick the lock."

Blade glances at me in surprise, but gestures for me to lead the way over. It's not a big deal, Jeff taught me to do loads of illegal and highly suspicious activities. From the time I was about fifteen, I could have broken into someone's house, assessed where they kept all their valuables and left again without anyone being any the wiser. Luckily for the world, I never developed a taste for that kind of life.

The door opens easily, and when I turn the handle, there's no wailing siren to tell anyone we've broken in. So far, so good. We creep into the warehouse. Directly in front of us are rows and rows of shelving units, all filled with neat stacks of wooden boxes, presumably helicopter parts. I search around, but still don't see any security cameras.

I frown over at Blade, and he shakes his head. He hasn't seen any either.

This situation is weird. It's starting to make me nervy, and that's never good on a mission. I take a breath, settle myself down and keep moving forward.

I use all my senses, including the spell web, to keep an eye on what's happening around me. I don't dare pull on the magic of the spell web, but I can use it like I always used to, as another sense that can tell me what's coming up. There are definitely supers ahead of us somewhere, in a large group.

Voices up ahead make me slow my pace. I peer around the end of the enormous shelving unit into an open space. It's filled with a range of different helicopters in various states of construction. Some with no rotors, some only just the frames. Others almost complete. There are big state-of-the-art machines set up around the room, some of them a storey high, obviously to help with the construction of the helicopters.

The voices are getting louder, and I realize that it's mainly just one voice, followed by another couple of voices.

We creep closer. There's a crowd of people standing around a slightly raised dais. My heart leaps into my chest. Up on the stage is Seth. He's looking down at an old, hunched-over, beaky-looking man wearing an ancient cloak covered in shiny black feathers.

Raven feathers. Ew. That's like me wearing dragon-hide trousers.

The more I learn about the Ravens, the more I dislike them.

There's one more person on the dais, a pretty woman about my age.

Something about the situation sets my nerves immediately on edge. "What are they doing?" I whisper.

Zane gives me an odd look. "What do you think?"

I look again. The old dude is reading from a book—a bible—and is standing between the other two... like in a church.

Everyone else is standing in front of them, like they're witnessing something.

It's a freaking wedding.

Oh, hell no. "He's getting married?"

40

"I'm sure it's not his choice," says Zane, nodding toward black-suited guards stationed around the dais.

My brain is whirling.

I can't think through what's happening in front of me.

Seth's getting married.

To someone other than me.

It doesn't matter that it might not be his choice. My brain is still exploding.

"... I now pronounce you Raven and wife...." The words filter into my brain, and I glance up again as the old Raven closes the old bible. "You may now kiss the bride."

Seth raises his eyebrows, but the old man gestures at the woman with his head.

My hands turn into fists at my side as he leans down and kisses her on the cheek. She smiles up at him like he's the moon and the stars. He just looks uncomfortable.

I growl. I can't help it. And not a small growl, a large angry dragon growl that echoes around the walls. Seth looks over at me, and his face is a mix of relief and panic that would have made me laugh if it had been any other situation.

Without thinking about it, I transform. My clothes rip, and I don't care that it's another set of clothes gone. My dragon form springs to life, fire forming in my throat even as my body enlarges around me. For the first time in a long time, I feel out of control, like my dragon form is something to be feared rather than loved. Heat vision makes everything seem bright and dramatic.

I growl again, smoke blowing out through my nostrils, and fire churns inside me, ready to disgorge on anyone who dares to confront me.

I blink, and the heat sensors switch back to normal vision.

Normal for a dragon. Everything is bright, clear, and sharp. I'm towering over the crowded room now, and I spot Evan standing at the front alongside Mike. Evan's looking up at me with a mixture of resentment and fear. I take a step toward him, snarling.

This is all his fault.

The people who were moments ago crowded around the ceremony are all running for cover behind the helicopters in various states of construction around the room.

As the room clears, I spot my father, Si, Carrick, and Elena at the front of the room as well.

Three guards, all dressed in black Kevlar, run up to me. They aim, but before they can let off their pointless bullets, I swipe out, letting all three of them fly through the air and knock into the concrete wall beside me. They drop to the floor with a satisfying thwack.

I look around and snarl again, smoke pouring out of my nostrils. They'll need to do something more than that to stop me. Walking forward, away from Blade, Zane, and

Hazel, I unfurl my wings, letting them beat into the air. Wind pushes out from them and blows around the room.

"Mei, you made it," says my dad, casually, like he was expecting me at any minute. I guess he was.

I stomp forward, my tail swishing behind me in agitation, glaring with everything inside me at the actors in this crazy melodrama in front of me. I feel like fire is coming out my eyes, I'm so mad.

"I told you she'd be pissed off," says Seth to no one in particular. There's something in his voice that says he's happy about it.

The old man on the dais is standing his ground, but he sends another five guards in my direction with a wave of his hand.

They come forward just like the other three, this time a little more warily. Arms raised, guns at the ready. They look like they think I'm going to be afraid of their efforts at controlling me. Supers in this age still aren't used to the idea of a dragon, the biggest, baddest supernatural there is. They think their guns will make a difference to me.

This time my growl rumbles deep in my stomach, sending vibrations along the floor. The men hesitate. At least they have more sense than the other ones.

I take a breath in and then release my fire, starting it off at a point just before the men. They all jump back, and the flames follow them as they retreat. I get closer to them than is comfortable, pushing them to retreat faster and faster.

One manages to get off a shot, and it hits me on the flank. I snarl and turn a jet of flames on him, burning him to a crisp right there. There's a communal gasp from the people who are hiding around the space, but I don't care. He shot first.

This is war. They're aiming to kill me. I'm done playing nice. Done pretending that I'm not as strong as I am.

Done letting others get away with kidnapping my friends and thinking they're going to get away with it.

The other four guards turn tail and run. The old man on the dais glares up at me like he thinks he's impervious to my flames. I swish my tail, turning my head to make sure I haven't overlooked anyone. There are people hiding, but the rest of the guards have retreated to a spot together behind the dais. I get the feeling they're planning something, but for the moment, I focus my attention on the old man. Lifting my lips into a snarl, I give him the benefit of my sharp teeth.

The young woman next to him screams and jumps behind Seth, like she thinks that will save her.

"Mei, it's okay. You're here now. We can sort this out," says Seth, raising his arms in a soothing manner.

I take my glare off the old man and turn it to Seth.

"I did mention that she might not be that cool with you marrying someone else, Seth," says Carrick mildly from one side of the dais. He's standing with my father and the others. The guards that were previously with them have deserted to the back of the room.

"Mei, I had to do it. They were threatening Mike's family. It doesn't mean anything," Seth is saying, holding his hands up. "You know that."

I snort out smoke through my nostrils and turn my head to the others, my father and Carrick. I raise an eyebrow. Couldn't they have done something to help him?

My father shrugs. "They were expecting us and had us outnumbered."

I glare at Elena. What is she, chopped liver?

"Not everyone was raised to fight like you, Mei," says Carrick. "Elena doesn't have the same instincts."

The old man steps forward, catching the corner of my eye. I turn back to him, curious what he might have to say.

He clears his throat like he thinks more of his importance than I do. "Dragon, you must cease and desist. We are on the same side. This marriage was only what the old texts called for. It's the only way to harness the power of a phoenix. A dragon would only break down the powers. He needs a good Raven girl to steer him."

Steer him? I glance at Seth, eyebrows raised.

He shrugs. "They were threatening Tracey and the kids. I had to bide my time until the rest of you arrived."

I growl. Seth's a phoenix, more powerful by ten than anyone else in this room. How could he not tell them to shove it where the sun don't shine?

Then I remember the fear on Tracey's face as I opened the cabinet. The Ravens are clearly a danger to her and the kids.

I guess—

"Watch out, Mei!" yells Seth, pointing to the back of the room. Two guards are holding up an enormous rocket launcher pointed directly at me.

The guard squeezes the trigger, and the missile is launched.

41

I roar, half anger, half panic. Can my dragon scales defend against a *missile*? What about the people who are here with me? Are they trying to just kill us all?

Leaping forward, I meet the missile halfway and grab it between my paws. It's buzzing like it's going to explode any second and my claws clench convulsively around the slick metal. Swinging my head around, I try to figure out the best direction to head. There're people everywhere I look—except up. Leaping into the air, I unfurl my wings, beating them frantically until I'm near the ceiling of the large warehouse. There's a row of tall windows, and I aim myself like a dart toward them, still holding the vibrating missile in my paws.

I smash through the glass windows, my tail whipping out behind me, and aim up.

That's the only thought in my head. Up. Away from all the people. The missile is still squirming like it's alive, and there's a red blinking light on one side. Suddenly it starts to beep continuously, and the light goes from blinking to steady.

Raising my paws up as high as they'll go, I fling the missile away from me, then dive down back toward the warehouse again.

Behind me, the missile explodes in a noise like ten thousand firecrackers going off all at once and sends a powerful blast of burning air that sends me uncontrollably tumbling through the air. I roll end over end, not sure whether I'm up or down. I can't fight it, and I'm frightened my wings are going to break, so I curl them in until it's like I'm a giant basketball on a downward bounce.

The spinning slows, and I finally get a sense of where I am. The ground is speeding toward me, and I flick my wings out, trying to use them to decrease my speed as I hurtle downward. It doesn't work. The ground is still looming faster and faster. I can't control my landing, and I'm heading straight for the highway next to the Raven warehouse. Cars are zipping by, unaware that I'm speeding straight for them. I desperately beat my wings against the momentum created by the missile's blast, but it's not enough.

I hit the ground hard, spinning and rolling across the tar seal of the road. I narrowly miss a truck with a picture of a puppy on it, and then slump to a halt in front of a car that's only just managed to stop right in front of me.

Inside my head, everything is still spinning. I open one eye, trying to think my way out of this, but nothing is working. Humans are getting out of their cars, walking up to me. I can't even imagine what kind of a strain this will put on the spell web.

The spell web.

I gather it around me, pulling it like a cloak to hide me.

"It's an elephant," says one of the bystanders.

"How did it get in the air like that?"

"Must've been that explosion just now."

"Probably flying overhead. In a helicopter maybe."

"Is it dead?"

"That's outrageous. Poor animal, being forced to fly by helicopter. I'm going to call our local councilman. That kind of thing shouldn't be allowed."

Someone walks up close to me and puts a hand on my flank. I can't help it, my scales ripple under the touch, and I jerk away.

"It's alive!" says a voice. "We have to find someone who can help it."

"I don't know. That was a pretty big fall. Surely it can't survive that?"

"Stand back, please. Coming through." The new voice is authoritative, like they're supposed to be here, and a dying elephant on the highway is of course their concern.

I open one eye and blink blearily at Seth. He's closely followed by my father, who's waving people back like there's some kind of health hazard.

"We'll need to cordon this area off," Seth is saying. "Thanks for your concern, but we have everything under control now."

"I'll be talking to my local representative about this. Elephants in helicopters shouldn't be allowed."

"What?" says Seth, startled.

"How else would an elephant land on the road like this?" asks the voice peevishly.

I'm curious how Seth's going to handle her, but he manages it like a pro. "Talking to your local councilman sounds like a great idea. But right now, the... uh... elephant needs a bit of room. Move back please, ma'am."

Inside I know I need to move, to get out of here, but I can't make my body obey me. Everything seems broken. I groan, hiding my head inside one wing.

As soon as my head touches the wing, I scream in pain. Something's wrong with my wing. I open my eyes and stare down at it. There's a bone sticking out from the main line of the wing. Blood is flowing out of the wound, and down over my body. I drag my head out and away, shaking blood splatter off me.

How am I going to get out of here? What help am I going to be with the demons if I can't fly?

What if this is permanent?

Another hand touches my flank, but this time gentle ripples of calm flow through me and I lean into the hand. Seth.

"It's going to be okay, Mei. Don't worry. You saved a lot of people just now. They're real grateful."

I nod numbly, the pain in my wing blocking off my ability to do anything else.

"Zane's changing, and then he's going to help carry you back into the Raven Technologies warehouse. Elena says she might be able to help you once we get you there," says Seth into my ear.

I feel the spell web tingle, a wave of energy reaching me a second or two before Zane arrives, landing nimbly next to me. I can hardly wait to hear what the humans in the cars think they just saw.

But when I open my eyes again, there's a weird fog forming around us, and the spell web is glowing. The humans don't seem to be paying any attention to Zane. Perhaps he looks like a truck to them? Or one of those forklifts?

I snort out a laugh, which turns into a groan of pain as the movement eats into my wing bone.

Come on, Mei, I need you to stand up. We have to get you out of here, says Zane.

"Perhaps it would be better for her to change back into her human form?" asks my father. "We could manage her more easily?"

"Have you seen that wing? It'll be excruciating," says Seth, shaking his head. "She's better off as a dragon. She'll heal faster, if nothing else."

Somehow Zane uses his arms to pull me to standing, and I look around, trying to get my bearings. I'm not actually that far from the Raven warehouse. I take a tentative step, then cry out as my broken wing hits the ground. Zane moves so that his wing fits under mine, and he uses it to keep mine up. He's holding onto my side, keeping me on my feet, as we stumble toward the warehouse.

Seth and my father follow closely on the other side, Seth murmuring reassurances under his breath at a level he knows I'll be able to hear.

I have to keep my gaze focused on the warehouse, blocking everything out. I can't think of anything else, worry about what might be happening in the building, or who we might find when we get back.

Where do we go in? I ask Zane.

Round the back. The big hangar doors.

I nod weakly, although I'm not sure I can make it that far. My vision is starting to feel a little murky, and my thoughts are tumbling through my head in an incoherent mix of past and present.

No focus at all anymore.

The doors are starting to weave in front of me. And then they start moving up, and I realize it was actually just the normal upward motion of the doors. Another dragon ducks below the doors and strides over to me, her blue-green scales rippling over her body. Elena.

I haven't seen her in dragon form since she first arrived with Carrick.

She takes my other side and helps Zane carry me into the hangar area. My head hangs low, my eyes are mostly closed. Inside there are groups of people standing around, but they all turn and stare when the three of us come into the space. There's a current of fear, but also curiosity and interest. It's an unusual sight in these times.

Mike moves closer to Seth and whistles under his breath. "She sure knows how to knock herself around, huh?" he says. "Remember how badly off she was when you visited?"

"She's awake," says Seth. "And can hear you."

"You're gonna be fine, Mei," says Mike in a different tone of voice.

What happened? I ask. *Where's the old dude?*

When you took off with the missile, we overpowered the guards, and the Augury was locked up for crimes against the community, says Elena. *Turns out he told the guards to kill you, no matter the cost to anyone else.*

What did I do to make him hate me like that?

He wanted Seth for his daughter.

That's it? But she could have been hurt by the missile too.

Turns out the guards didn't understand the nuances of his instructions. They didn't realize he wouldn't want his own daughter killed.

I let out a breath and try not to let the pain in my wing knock me unconscious. It feels like I should be awake for every moment that's happening right now.

Elena and Zane help me to an area to one side of the room, and I collapse down onto the ground before my feet completely turn to Jell-O beneath me. Carrick comes to stand next to me, and I flinch away, growling. He'll want to take this wound, and I don't want to give it to him.

Tell him it's my wound to take, I say to Elena.

What makes you think I can communicate with him in this form? asks Elena carefully.

Of course you can. I don't have time for you to pretend with me, I snap back.

Elena blinks, then nods slowly. *I have told him.*

Can you help me? Or do I have to do this on my own? The pain is driving me out of my head. I remember the healing I did when I fell out of the sky when I was learning to fly. I almost killed Seth and Si in the process.

I can help you. I can't heal you completely, but I can make you more comfortable.

I nod, and suddenly my head is too heavy for me to hold up. I lower it to the ground as the world starts to spin, and I close my eyes. Seth comes closer and puts one arm along my flank. A sob works its way up my throat at the feeling of desperation he's giving off.

"Stay strong, Mei," he says. "I can't lose you."

Help me, I whisper to Elena.

She moves closer and puts her paw on my shoulder. The spell web surges around us, thickening over my skin, wrapping me in a dense cover of magic. Tingles spread over my whole body, and I feel weightless, like the spell web is drawing out anything of substance inside me.

I'm struggling to hold onto my thoughts, to understand where I am and what's going on.

And then I black out.

42

I wake slowly, testing out my body piece by piece and feeling kinda pissed off about how often I seem to be passing out recently. The wing is still stiff, but it doesn't hurt anymore. I open an eye. Seth's sleeping next to me in a chair, and we're still in the same warehouse as before. Night filters in from the broken windows above. Helicopters are like strange statues around us, and people are wandering past on their way to somewhere important.

Seth stirs and lifts his head.

"Good to see you, sleepyhead," he says. "I was worried about you."

Good to be alive.

Without thinking, I lower my head and nuzzle into him, and he puts one hand up and along my neck.

"Ah, you're awake," says my father, striding toward me. "Elena says you'll be able to change back into your human form in a few hours. But in the meantime, we need to catch up."

I nod, not sure what he's so worried about.

"The demons are still swarming," he says without preamble.

My head hitches up sharply. I'd forgotten about the demon swarm, the original reason we flew all this way.

"Yes. That was my reaction too. It seems there really is a problem. A big one. They thought they saw where things were going. The Augury admitted to me that he made a deal with a man named Connor McKenzie."

I growl under my breath and look around for Hazel and Blade. Does my father know who Connor is?

"Connor's not a good guy," continues Damien. "He's an old enemy of Hazel's."

I settle back down. As usual, my father knows everything already.

"He's been feeding them a bunch of lies to get them to help him. But all they've managed to do is create a plague of demons in Newport News."

Dad hesitates. "We're about to head out to battle the demon infestation. And you have to stay here, Mei. We need to deal with them right now. And you're not well enough to fight them."

All the ridges along my back rise up, and my mouth lifts up into a snarl. I shake my head slowly at him. Never. I won't let them battle the demons without me.

"Don't worry, Mei, this is only a small number compared to the army of demons that Connor is amassing on the West Coast. You'll be able to help us fight them soon enough."

I shake my head. I won't let them do it.

"You're not indispensable, Mei," my father says calmly. "We have two other dragons, both older and much more experienced than you. Sergei is flying in as well. Not to mention that Hazel was born for this. She could probably take on all the demons on her own."

I look down at Seth.

"Ah, yes, we'll need our trusty phoenix. He fights alongside the dragons against the demons."

A shiver clatters across my scales, and I glare around me. Everyone I love is here, and they're all about to go out and fight creatures that I'm not entirely sure can be killed.

Certainly not by anything that will usually kill a human or a super. How do they plan to do it? What methods have they found? What if Hazel can't control them like she controlled the one in the lab?

"It'll be fine, Mei. You need to stay here and rest. We'll deal with the infestation and be back before you know it." He stands up and places one hand on my arm. "You need to get yourself better. You've already done more for this whole situation than you realize by destroying the missile. The people saw firsthand the deviousness of their Augury and the selflessness of a dragon."

I settle reluctantly back on my haunches. I glance back over my shoulder at my wing, but it's still red and swollen. Pain tingles along the edges, and I know I can't fly.

Trying to insist on it is just stupid.

I nod my head once.

"We'll be back before you know it," says Dad. "Come on, Seth. Let's go."

Seth stands up. He turns back to me. "We'll get everything sorted out... including...." He glances to one side in the direction of the empty dais.

I blow smoke out my nostrils at him. *I'm still annoyed you agreed to marry someone else.*

Seth waves the smoke out of his face. "Okay, I deserve that."

Where is your wife anyway? I look around, trying to spot her among the people loitering in small groups.

"She's going to come with us, help with fighting the demons," says Seth.

I growl. *She gets to go, and I have to stay here?*

"She's a good person," says Seth, raising his hands, palms up. "She's just as much a victim of her father as I was."

Fire starts to rumble in my stomach, and smoke emerges out my mouth.

My father steps in front of Seth. "We'll have time to sort this out properly when we get back. Right now, we have some demons to face. And you have to rest." He pats me with one hand, and then drags Seth away by the arm. Seth looks back over his shoulder, his expression concerned.

But he still goes with my dad and leaves me here.

I watch as the group packs up and leaves, Elena and Zane carrying three people apiece. My father, Carrick, Si, Hazel, and Blade, plus the girl. Seth turns into his phoenix form next to them, and they all take off into the night. I hear a strange buzzing noise from outside, but I can't even turn my head enough to figure out what it is.

I slump back down onto my belly and put my head onto my front paws. What am I going to do about Seth? What if Si was right, all that time ago? What if there really is some rule that says a phoenix should marry a Raven girl?

Where does that leave me?

Does he want to be married to her? He defended her to me, that means he must at least like her. It's probably a hassle being with someone like me, the center of attention, constantly having people attack and trying to kill me.

Maybe he wants people to look at him because he's a gorgeous phoenix, not because he's with the crazy dragon girl?

I lie on the floor, my thoughts tumbling around inside

me like a kaleidoscope being turned by an enthusiastic toddler. I can't seem to settle on one, and they're turning too fast for me to even understand most of them.

"Hello, Mei," says a familiar voice behind me.

I sit up and turn my head. Surely I heard that wrong?

But I didn't. It's Director Holden.

What the hell is he doing here?

43

Beside the director is a small group of burly men, including Evan.

I frown down at them, not quite understanding what's happening. I'm not worried, until a square metallic device is brought out from behind the director by one of his goons.

One of the Earthbound's machines. A vision of Tarsal writhing on the ground fills my head. I try to sit up and a sharp flash of pain from my wing goes through my whole body.

A suited man presses the button on the side, and it whirrs into life.

My head still feels fuzzy, and the pain from my wing is making me tremble. I look around desperately, but the hangar seems to have emptied of people.

"Evan did a fine job of sending everyone home," says the director. "There's no one else here to save you, little dragon girl."

The machine warms up slowly, but I can already feel the

terrible scratching as it does what it's designed to do—forcibly turn me back into my human form.

Except this time with my newly broken bones, it's excruciating. I scream, a half human, half dragon sound that reverberates around the room.

"That's the most delightful sound I've heard in a long time, Mei. Certainly the best sound I've heard since I discovered that you'd gotten Liling killed."

I can hardly hear what he's saying, the torture of the transformation is so intense. This is exactly why Elena said not to transform. Except I'm already halfway healed so I can't imagine the horrors of changing just after the injury.

"Grab her," says the director, pointing to me.

I'm lying on the floor, my arm out at a strange angle, unable to move or protest or even kick out at them as they grab me and drag me along the floor.

"Bag her," says the director. "Then we're getting out of here."

Two of the men bind my legs and hands, shove a gag over my mouth, then push me into an enormous black sports bag—like something ice hockey players might use—and lift it up between them. I can't even fight them, even though everything inside me wants to do it. I'm still too weak.

The spell web vibrates over my body, waiting for me to use it. If I do, it'll knock me out. I'll only have one chance. I have to make it work.

I let the power of the spell web fill me up, holding off, waiting for the perfect moment. It froths with magic, burning and buzzing to get out. The power expands, bursting out of me, and I send it out over the grid lines. I don't think, I just push it out, a surge of magic that will knock everyone around me out. The magic is like lightning, a loud, bright, burst of energy. For a second there's silence, and then I hear the sound of bodies dropping around me. I can't see anything through the bag, but it must have worked.

My heart lifts, even as I feel the feedback coming back at me, the terrible reverberation of the spell web's energy that is the prequel to another attack.

And then two hands grab me through the material of the bag. "Thought you'd get us, eh?" says a voice in my ear. "The director was prepared for you."

I squeeze my eyes shut against the pain of the spell web attack and try to understand why he's not knocked out like the others.

There's only one explanation. He must be human and completely unaffected by the spell web. I don't know what they think they're seeing, or how their brains explained a dragon that turned into a human, but they know enough to keep going while the supers are all knocked out.

Two men lift me up, and I start to shake. The backlash is already starting. Lights are flashing in front of my eyes.

"Pick up the director, make it look like he's just unwell. Leave the Raven informer, we don't need him."

They walk toward the exit, their gait casual, as if everything is normal. I don't know what they're trying to pass a large black bag off as, but I can't do anything to stop them. The pain is increasing, the attack intensifying, and I don't think I'm going to be conscious for much longer.

"Hey there," says a familiar voice. My heart leaps. Mike is still here. He must have been far enough away to avoid the spell web blast. Maybe he'll notice something's off. Pain runs along my body, like those fire ants are biting my skin in a fight for survival.

"Hello," says one of the men carefully.

The two men carrying me come to a halt.

"Where're you going?"

"Just taking the SIG director out to his car. He's feeling unwell."

"He can't leave until the others get back," says Mike sternly.

"Understood. We'll be just outside." The man's voice sounds reasonable, and he's probably indicating the director, who'll be drooping like a daisy off someone. I try to move, to do something to let Mike know I'm in the bag. But I'm starting to sink into oblivion, the pain overriding all my senses. All I can do is scream on the inside.

Mike hesitates. "Okay, sure. Good idea."

We move off again, and my hopes curl into a ball inside me.

The cool night air hits me. We're outside already, and no one has stopped them. Panic flares, like a fire inside my belly, spreading up through my torso. Everyone who knows me is off fighting demons. My movements are too slow and sluggish, but my swelling panic helps me to finally start struggling. The spell web surrounds me, and I let it seep into me, strengthening me even as it causes a spasm of agony to roll through my body. I kick out at one of my captors, and he grunts in pain.

Then he punches me in the stomach in retaliation. I gasp for breath, blackness seeping into my mind, so far gone that I've almost forgotten where I am and what's happening. The spell web buzzes in agitation.

"Stay still if you want to live," says one of the guards.

I doubt I'm going to live if I stay still either. The director just wants the power of the spell web at his command. If he can find a way to get it out of me, he will.

Maybe that's what this is all about? Maybe he's found a way?

I try to struggle again, but this time my movements are weaker. My broken arm feels like the bone might have busted through the wound again, and tears fall down my cheeks as I try to ignore the pain and fight back anyway.

If they steal me away, how am I going to work with Hazel? How are we going to solve the mystery of my attacks? How are we going to *save me*?

As they dump me in the back of a car, and the trunk lid descends on me, buzzing blackness descends over me as my body gives up.

44

It's been a long time since they dumped me in this room.

I don't know how long.

Days maybe.

Weeks.

It could be years, I don't know.

The room is holding my powers in check, muffling the spell web, making my dragon abilities disappear. It's like the Earthbound box, except all around me. They've somehow managed to take the original technology and expand on it.

Something is affecting my senses. I feel like there's fluffy cotton everywhere inside my head. I don't know how they're doing this to me, but I really wish they'd stop.

I don't know where the others are, or whether they were able to defeat the demons. I don't know if they're trying to get me out of here, or if they think I'm dead.

I think the only reason I'm still alive is that the director wants the spell web, and he'll do anything to get it.

I curl up on the metal bed, bringing my knees up to my

chest, and wrap my arms around my knees. I don't know how much longer I can take this.

The lock in the door on the other side of the room clicks. The big metal doors slowly open, and two men walk in.

The first one is Connor McKenzie, who's visited me before. He likes to gloat and then in the same breath cajole and convince. He's been trying to get me to work for him since I arrived... here. Wherever here is.

The second man steps out from behind Connor, and everything inside me freezes. His pitiless dark eyes pierce into mine. The Man in Black stands beside Connor, a smirk on his face as he stares down at me.

This is my worst nightmare and I don't know how I'm going to survive.

**

Thanks for reading Cursed Dragon. I hope you enjoyed it!

Warrior Dragon, the final book in the series will be out soon!

In the meantime, I have exciting news - if you liked Hazel from **Cursed Dragon,** you'll love my other series - **The Demon Hunter in Hiding series.**

It's the story of how Hazel went from an inmate at an insane asylum to demon hunter extraordinaire!

Turn the page to find out more...

Thank you!

It's so awesome to see you at the end of another one of my books. I hope you enjoyed Cursed Dragon!

I have some exciting news - if you liked Hazel from **Cursed Dragon,** you'll love my new series - **Demon Hunter in Hiding.** It's the story of how Hazel went from being a nerdy researcher to a kick-butt demon hunter...

About Secrets & Demons

To look at me, you wouldn't think my whole life is a lie.

By day, I'm a nerdy researcher who likes to design inventions. At night, I hunt monsters.

Yep. I said it. Monsters. They're real, and they're out there.

Turn the page to get an exclusive excerpt from Hazel's first book.

Brand new series linked to the Dragon Rising series!

Secrets & Demons Excerpt

Standing in Dr. Green's office, I'm more scared than I've ever been in my life—and that's saying something, given the monsters I've seen.

But Dr. Green *is* a kind of monster.

In the eight months since I arrived at the Ravenwood Mental Health Facility for Violent Offenders, Dr. Green has always been composed and controlled—her straight, white-blonde hair in a perfect asymmetrical cut, her makeup always smoothly applied, never a wrinkle on her power suits. She's the ultimate elegant ice queen. Even the thin, pale line of a scar down one side of her face has always seemed somehow delicate and precious, rather than irregular.

But now, everything's changed.

For a start, she's almost unrecognizable—hair loose, clothes rumpled, eyes wild. She's completely unravelled. Standing in the middle of her office, her sharp heels pressing carelessly into the scattered pieces of paper that used to be neatly stacked reports on her desk, she's looking down at me like I'm an insect she'd like to crush.

Someone just arriving might think she'd been robbed, or maybe that a fight had broken out in her office. But it's Dr. Green who's been systematically destroying her own office in a demented rage.

And it's all directed at me.

Needless to say, I'm shaking so hard I can barely stand.

Especially since I'm being held secure by two burly uniformed orderlies—Frankie and Marlon—who are standing on either side of me, both stiff with matching resentment. My hair is falling over my face in long scraggly brown strands, and all I want to do is push it back, but they're holding me firmly in place. No mercy for me today.

"You might have helped your friends escape, Hazel, but *you* will never leave Ravenwood," Dr. Green says, her voice low and vindictive. Her scar is a hard white against the angry red on her cheeks. "I'll make sure of it."

Cold seeps over my whole body, and I finally begin to understand the full ramifications of what I've done. I let out a strangled noise, despite my determination not to give her the satisfaction. What was I thinking? Why did I let them escape without me? I thought Dr. Green was vile *before*— now, she's going to be pure evil.

Some kind of instinct—like a mouse who's been trapped by a cat—makes me glance furtively around, looking for a way out. The main door behind me is guarded, and the only other door goes into Dr. Green's secret lair where she hides all the notes from her illegal research. No safety for me there. The windows at the back of her large desk are locked down tight, and the guards would stop me as soon as I moved an inch.

But I still check. I can't help myself. Even when I know there's no way I'm getting out of here.

"Keep your eyes focused on me, Hazel. Listen closely," says Dr. Green. This time she's using her cool therapist's voice. I can sense the effort it's costing her to be so composed.

I try to do as she commands, but it's difficult to look at her directly. It's like she's so sharp, it'll hurt my eyes if I do.

I shift in place, trying desperately to figure out a way out of this. Except I can't think properly. All I can concentrate on is the fact that Frankie and Marlon are holding on to my arms too tightly, and I can't even complain about the bruises I'm going to have. I tricked them both when I helped my friends Poppy and Daphne escape, and they know Dr. Green will take the escape out on them as well as me.

"Marlon, you say she was out in the hallway?" she asks, for about the millionth time.

"Yes, Dr. Green. Looked real suspicious." Marlon nods his head in his usual efficient way, as if he hasn't already answered the same question a million times.

Usually both Frankie and Marlon aren't that bad. They look burly and menacing, but I've helped them both at various times, using my ability to fix almost anything to make their lives easier. Frankie's always looked after me, keeping me out of Dr. Green's way if he can. He even smuggled me a box of chocolates from his mom when I fixed her iPod. Marlon took longer to respond to my brand of charm —it was only when I fixed the coffee machine in the staff room that he finally started to talk to me like a person and not a patient.

Now as I glance at them out of the corner of my eye, they're both staring straight ahead, deep matching scowls on their faces. They're pissed at me for my betrayal. After everything they did for me, I brought the wrath of Dr. Green down on them.

But that doesn't mean I feel sorry for them. At least they get to go home to their families at night. I'm going to be trapped here, trying to survive whatever Dr. Green decides to throw at me. She has complete control over everything I do. And I mean *everything*.

What I eat.

Who I talk to.

Where I sleep.

When I sleep.

Everything.

Ravenwood is where they send people who've been judged defective in some way, considered too dangerous to live on the outside. Once you've been sent to Ravenwood, there's no going back. It becomes a giant black mark on your official records, a shameful blot that will allow them to make the same judgements against you, again and again, even if you manage to somehow get out.

Once you're at Ravenwood, they prefer to lock you up and throw away the key. Of course, I only discovered all this once I was here.

"I know you were involved, Hazel," continues Dr. Green. "Neither Poppy nor Daphne would be able to plan something like this."

Another half-sob works its way up from my chest. She's right. I planned the whole escape. I figured out how to open the door in the staff room when I fixed the coffee machine. I found a way to get us out of the communal TV room by creating a distraction. I gathered the information we needed so we could make the attempt on the perfect day. I was supposed to leave with Poppy and Daphne today, not be trapped here like a fucking mouse.

And it was Marlon who ruined the plan by taking a damn restroom break when he should have been somewhere else. It's lucky he's a whistler, or we would've all been caught. In that moment during the escape, as his heavy tread came closer and closer to the staff room, I knew the only way for Daphne and Poppy to get out of here was for me to distract him. It was either *some* of us, or *none* of us.

Right this minute, with Dr. Green breathing her metaphorical fire at me, I wish I hadn't fallen on my sword so quickly. But in the moment, it seemed like the only decision I could make. Daphne was in much greater danger from Dr. Green than I was.

So here I am, facing Dr. Green and whatever she decides to throw at me. Trying not to regret my actions, and hoping against hope I'll be able to find another hole in their security, the same way I found the first one.

"Tell me where they went, and I might be more lenient," says Dr. Green, her voice soft, like she's trying to pretend she's not already planning how she's going to make me pay for this.

I shake my head, but I can't force any words past the thickness in my throat. I jerk my arm reflexively, trying to hide my tears. Marlon tightens his grip even more as if he thinks I'm trying to escape again. *If only I could.*

There's no one to stop Dr. Green from punishing me however she likes. For her, it's not about the escape of two supposedly dangerous prisoners. I've spent enough time with her over the last few months to know she doesn't really care that Poppy and Daphne are out there in the world. She's not worried about protecting innocent people from supposedly violent offenders, or even helping her vulnerable patients. What's got her so furious is that it's ruined her perfect record. We've hit her where it hurts—in her cherished reputation, her inflamed ego, her warped pride.

Despite everything, I don't regret what happened. Poppy and Daphne are finally free of this woman's control. Daphne was about to be transferred to Ward D, which is worse than a death sentence for an inmate at Ravenwood. It's the place where Dr. Green tests her experimental drugs and illegal treatments. Sometimes they work, sometimes they don't.

Patients in Ward D end up in chronic pain, some with missing limbs or mysterious scars, others blind or deaf. There are horrible rashes, strange reactions, and many so far gone they can barely tell you their name, let alone string a sentence together. I've visited Ward D twice—both times to fix something—and I never want to go back there.

Because of me, Daphne's no longer headed for Ward D. That thought sends a tiny sliver of happiness soaring in my stomach. I saved them. At least she's free.

Unlike me.

"Do you want to know something about me, Hazel?" Dr. Green is speaking conversationally. "I'm considered an expert witness in the justice system. Judges bring me in when they need help determining the mental state of a patient."

I stare at her, unblinking. I already know this. It's how she got me transferred here without even a whisper of a trial for murder.

"I'm friends with the judges, Hazel. And if I tell them to, they will let me keep you here for the rest of your life," Dr. Green snarls, finally giving up pretending to be nice. "I'll get you registered as criminally insane. After everything that went on at your survivalist community, it'll be easy. I'll tell the judge on your case that you're so far inside your para-normal delusions, there's no way back, and I'll get you officially diagnosed with the most severe form of paranoid schizophrenia possible. You'll never get out of here. *Ever.*" By the time she finishes speaking, her face is a putrid shade of red and the veins are sticking out on her neck like drainpipes.

My vision blurs as I watch her lose it in front of me. I try to tell myself that she's just ranting. That it won't really be like that. Someone from Elk Creek will come find me here. Baz will get me out if no one else will. Surely somewhere in my distant future, there's the possibility of me being outside of Ravenwood and away from Dr. Green?

The problem is, I believe her every word. She's the kind of person who knows how to get what she wants. Eight months ago, she convinced a judge I was too mentally unstable to stand trial for the murder of my parents, and she had me sent here, under her care. I wasn't allowed to prove I didn't do it, and no one ever believed me when I said I would never hurt my mom and dad.

If she doesn't want me to ever leave Ravenwood, that's it.

I'm done. This is going to be my life.

I try not to let it break me apart.

"I'll make sure you never see the light of day again," she vows, almost as if she can tell what I'm thinking.

I feel a sizzle of energy, and it's like her vow has released something into the air around us. She's going to make sure I suffer for this; I know it down to my very bones. I slump down even further and try to keep my tremors to a minimum. I chose this. I decided to stay so the others could escape. I'm not going to let her see me cry.

Much.

"Say something, girl," she screeches at me, her spittle landing on the floor at my feet. The veins in her neck now look like they're about to pop out of her skin.

"I... I didn't...," I croak out, stuttering to a stop when I see the wildness in her eyes. I've never seen her this unhinged, not in all our sessions, in all the times I've made her angry over the last few months.

"Don't lie to me!" She picks a vase up off the sideboard and aims it like she's going to throw it at my face. I can't even duck out of the way with Frankie and Marlon holding me tight between them. I flinch as she launches the vase, but it misses me—and Frankie and Marlon—and smashes against the wall behind us. "You're never going to leave this place, you hear me?"

I nod jerkily.

"You're the key to my research, Hazel. You always have been. You're the one who's going to help me find the missing pieces. I *was* going to go slowly, to test things on the others before I got to you. But not anymore. Now I'm going to put you at the top of the list. You're being moved to Ward D effective immediately."

I hear Frankie's soft intake of breath over the buzzing noise that's filling my brain. I'm part of her research? She was going to take it slowly? *Ward D?*

My stomach is so tight with fear that the pain is radiating out over my whole body, but I need to know more. "What research? Why me?" I say, my words raw and cracking in the middle.

"You're unique, Hazel," says Dr. Green with an unpleasant smile. "Not like the rest of them. Your visions make you special."

"If I'm so special, why send me to Ward D to die?" The words fall out of my mouth without asking permission from my brain. I'm completely vulnerable to her whims and it terrifies me.

"Don't worry, I won't let you die. At least not right away," says Dr. Green with vindictive relish, the whites of her eyes clearly visible. "I'm going to keep you alive long enough to finish my research and prove my theories. Long enough for me to find a way to make up for my sister's death." Dr. Green's expression is so unhinged, I don't think she's even aware of what she just said.

"Your sister?" I repeat aloud. I've never heard her mention a sister before. I'd assumed she didn't have a family, that maybe she lived in a small hut on the Ravenwood grounds with a cauldron and a black cat.

But she's done talking. "Take her away," she snarls with a flick of her wrist, and Frankie and Marlon drag me out the door and toward my doom.

Check out Secrets & Demons on your favorite retailer now!

Hi! My name's Trudi Jaye and I've got a secret.

A secret society, that is.

Especially designed for people like you who love reading my books, the Trudi Jaye Secret Society is a place filled with magic and laughter, and most of all... free stories.

Everyone who joins the society is given access to an ancient tome full of the stories, novellas, bonus epilogues, and deleted scenes from all the different Trudi Jaye series.

Called **The Shadow Archives,** you can access it by clicking the link below, and joining the secret society...

Join Trudi Jaye's Secret Society... if you dare!

www.trudijayewrites.com/shadow-archives

Books by Trudi Jaye

Dragon Rising Series

Lost Dragon (Prequel Novella available via the Trudi Jaye Secret Society)

Hidden Dragon

Searching Dragon

Fighting Dragon

Cursed Dragon

Warrior Dragon (coming soon)

Demon Hunter in Hiding Series

Dreams & Demons (Prequel Novella available via the Trudi Jaye Secret Society)

Secrets & Demons

Agents & Demons

Magic & Demons

Dragons & Demons

Spells & Demons

Elemental Witch Series (With Tania Hutley)

The Trouble with Magic

The Problem with Witches

The Danger with Demons

Firecaller Series

Salt (Prequel Novella available via the Trudi Jaye Secret Society)

Subtle Knife (Prequel Novella available via the Trudi Jaye Secret Society)

Fire Mage

Royal Mage (coming soon)

Dark Carnival Series

The First Ever Wish (Prequel Novella available via the Trudi Jaye Secret Society)

If Magic Were Wishes

The Gift

Magic for Lost Souls (available via the Trudi Jaye Secret Society)

High Flyer

Hidden Magic

The Shadow Prophecy

Hi! I'm Trudi Jaye and I'm the author of this book.

I'm from New Zealand, where I currently live on a beautiful rural property surrounded by horses and cows (not mine!) with my lovely husband and my cheeky tween daughter.

I've been writing since I was a kid, and for ten years I worked as a magazine writer and editor, on topics ranging from hardware and electronics to holidays, recipes and university-level research projects.

Now I write novels full time.

I enjoy yoga, although I'm not very bendy, and karate, although I don't like the idea of hitting anyone.